Let the Scaffolds Fall

stories
by Shaun Rouser

ROADSIDE PRESS

Dedicated, above all, to the truth that one of the hardest things in life is not, as the cliché says, letting go, but grasping what should be let go of.

Table of Contents

Inheritance

He was nearing the end of his life. The body, always a banality, was now a millstone. Rising from bed to empty his bladder, for instance, required he recruit his mind with an intensity that had been reserved for genuine work, such that swinging his feet to the floor was like an act of telekinesis. Then he'd move with less haste than his bladder demanded. Minding the back that would not straighten, the knees that refused to bend. The final cliché: clutching sink and wall, he would lower himself to the toilet, releasing spurts and drips which thankfully no longer missed. But with age the body weakened, and because it happened gradually, there were signposts on the road marking stages of diminishment. One ascended stairs slower, as an example, before avoiding the task altogether. What could not be prepared for were the deaths of others. No one died then everyone did with sudden regularity. His grandparents passed while he was a young man, but they had always existed in a state of agedness to him, so their deaths felt less consequential. It was decades more until someone near to him died: his parents went, mom then dad, in their old age within a couple of years of each other. But unlike his grandparents, their deaths were different. Their mortality made death possible. A friend of four decades was killed when his flight to Mexico City crashed in a Southwestern desert. The husband of his sister went to bed one evening and never returned. His daughter, a physician like the rest of her family, miscarried his namesake. His wife died and he was certainly next.

He woke from a recurrent dream in which he was in a room,

lighted enough to see its darkness, a fetid, nauseating odor trapped in his mouth and nose. His arms were raised, and as he walked cautiously, terror-struck, his weak hands clutched in vain for unseen walls or doors. He lay in bed, picturing his wide open eyes, their sinking farther into his head each day. They were a no man's land between his mole-covered nose and withered forehead, holes and hillocks left by mortar fire. His mouth was dry. With predictable effort, he rose in bed and maneuvered his feet to the floor. Wool socks kept them warm year-round. Ten miniature Bloodhounds set out, wiggling and probing the hardwood, finding his sheepskin moccasins just before he turned on the bedside lamp. In the bottom drawer of his nightstand, alongside batteries, a flashlight, a whistle, and first aid kit, was a watch.

From childhood, his mother called herself Henry. This was her father's name, and the distance between it and Henrietta was unbearable. She imagined him larger than his five-feet-six inches, but her reality filled the expanses of his dreams. Henry was his tiny apostle, and despite living in an inhospitable region of the twentieth century, they believed she'd be a doctor someday, too. She did, in fact, and carried herself from grade school onward with obvious self-assurance. Like countless before her (those who loved their labor but more often those who did not), Henry also died after work. On her way out, Henry Peoples, née Gaynor, told a colleague, "Good night," words recorded by history as her last. Then died between sixty-thirty pm and seven—torso crumpled in the trunk of her car, legs dangled over its bumper. Her heart resigned without notice. Near Henry's right hand was a pair of sneakers, the "more comfortable shoes" worn before and after work, and on her left wrist a decades-old anniversary gift. Her widower was as maddened by the watch's invulnerable tic as he was devastated by the death of his wife. It reminded him that life continued whether the love of that life was alive or not. He gave the hellish keepsake to his eldest as though it were the British crown and spent his remaining years withdrawing slowly into death. But his passing was less surprising than Henry's. Following the men in his family, he was morose and antisocial his last years on earth before dying in proximity to a bathroom. Collapsing midway, digestively so, between kitchen and toilet, washing jam-stained fingers in his case. And as family members before them had, his mourning children also greeted his death with unvoiced relief. He was a different person in later years, they reflected, so in the company of others, they remembered earlier, better times. Cornell Peoples II was a beloved colleague and physician, a devoted father and husband, the first to earn a degree in his family, and most importantly, a keeper of their last name from birth.

A younger self would have moved through his house without a light. But he was older, less confident and familiarity with each hallway and corner provided no comfort. One could fracture his shoulder against a doorframe, shatter his toes walking into a couch. The bedroom light joined the bedside lamp, the hallway lit up an exhibit of pictures on both walls. That corridor, the first bookshelf he passed, like the rest of his home, contained items saved because during the objects' more enduring lives they'd passed through the hands of someone he loved. Among his books, a slim volume jutted out more in his mind than in reality. He was not a literary man. He never read Nabokov.

Ty was a patient before they became friends—their bond from that first meeting a shared love of debate. His ailment: ferocious, years-long spasms in his chest; its cause, then as it would be the remainder of his life: uncompromising anxiety. Ty harbored the adolescent desire to leave his country, but as he greyed, this longing moderated into an aging man's wish to see the world before dying. He'd traveled to California twice, San Francisco and LA via bus, taken a train to New York City but never boarded a plane. Mexico City was close, he said, and a bilingual dictionary would get him through eight days with his energetic but iffy Spanish. The night before his flight he called, chest spasms, and they spoke until it abated. Seated next to a window, Ty worked longhand on his long-unfinished novel until the plane began to plummet, scribbling diagonal, blue cursive in a notepad. The plane rattled and began to fall, their oxygen masks deployed, a flight attendant ordered everyone to buckle up. His chest spasmed and tormented him as it hadn't before, as if the muscles were launching a final assault to defeat him. He shuttered the window with preternatural calm. The trip from mundane to tragedy was no more than sixty seconds. On the first day of the search, his body was found, still shackled to part of his seat. *Transparent Things*, Ty's favorite, had been borrowed months before, the hopeful promise to read it unfulfilled.

At the living room's threshold, he stopped, felt along the wall for a light switch but could not find one. He could visualize the pearl-white Sheetrock, furniture, paintings, knickknacks, pictures … Taking a guarded step inside, he clutched at the wall and became more horrified with each futile handful. He paused, slowing his breaths, clawed at the wall again. Again. Again. Again. With more panic than memory, he attacked the doorframe's other side. The switch materialized beneath his hands and he reassured himself time had not made him a stranger in his home. He'd always remembered its location. In the light, he saw walls stained with sweat from his palms, a birthday card had fainted on a nearby curio's top shelf. Before leaving the room, he helped the patient to its feet.

To his sister, Nadine, he was a faithful yet disinterested brother, supporting her with everything but undivided attention. Their lives were connected in history but unlinked in the present: Thom, her partner, had especially lived in the hinterlands of his memories. When Nadine announced their engagement, in the solitude of his feelings he reacted with bemused surprise and disgrace. A man he knew little about was marrying a woman he should have known better. Life, however, could be funny, forgiving. It had brought Thom into the Peoples family and, before that, given him the birthday February 12, the same as Lincoln and Darwin. Showing his affection, he unfailingly sent Thom birthday cards honoring their legacies, inscribing them all, "They belong to the ages." Thom responded, sending cards March 23, the birthday he shared with JM Peebles. "One man's quack is another man's genius. See you at 100!" Their family tradition lasted until Thom's death. As Nadine recounted that day, they had breakfast, went to work, returned home for dinner. Afterwards they talked in the living room before Thom completed his nighttime routine of deep breathing exercises and light stretches. Lying on his stomach with blankets pulled to his chin, Thom was in bed when she joined him, dying in that position before sunrise.

He entered the kitchen and stopped at the table. Leaning against a chair with both hands, waiting until he'd gathered himself enough to reach the sink. Three cotton placemats remained. His daughter, Wesley, sewed them when she was fourteen. Red for him, green for her, yellow for her mother. They were decorations unchanged by time, which marked their unchanging positions at the kitchen table. Wesley's high chair had been placed exactly where she sat as a high schooler, as a young woman returning from college, as an adult visiting her aging parents. Sitting there, she told them of her pregnancy, the child who'd be her first. And they knew, without her having to say, a girl would be named Cornelia. Months later Wesley told her parents she knew what her symptoms meant, that when your body revolts, medical knowledge is worse than useless because with it there is no hope. Had she been able to believe, the baby would have lived a few hours longer in her mind. He poured a glass of warm water from the faucet and sat, licking and wiping ungovernable droplets from his chin and lips, then continued sitting as he had for decades, in the place where he drank his coffee, ate his eggs, read his papers. Nowadays, those papers were different. He no longer read two or three local dailies because just one shabby publication existed and even the national papers were haggard twins to their former selves. Complaints were made, subscriptions cancelled. Over breakfast, he now preferred reading alt weeklies because they were free and interesting. His care aide gathered them during her commute. Following the death of his wife, daily help was a compromise with his daughter. She suggested an assisted living community and he demanded to live alone in his house. The counter was close enough to grab a paper from his current pile. He had to pee. As with many of the body's demands, it was nonexistent then urgent. He stood, but passing into the living room, tiring, he ignored his bladder and listened to his lungs. Hunched over, one hand on his knee, the other grabbing a cheap table, mismatched with the rest of their furniture.

Melinda had bought it during the last years of her dying days: she needed another place for messages. A mutual friend introduced them five decades earlier. From that first meeting, when she wrote her address in the margins of a coupon, he felt her affection in the notes she left behind. She attached them to doors, television screens, rearview mirrors, on tile behind the shower head, she taped letters to the handle of his briefcase—wherever he would find them. They were I-love-yous but also questions she forgot to ask, observations that didn't need responses, calls to finish grocery lists. He kept them all, first in shoeboxes then a safe—from coupon to last, barely legible reminder to herself. With old age, the notes became more numerous and mundane. In her disintegrating cursive, a Post-it was placed on the front door that said, "Remember to lock." A sheet of typed paper, taped to the kitchen counter, listed in which drawers and cabinets to find silverware and plates. Melinda had pinned mnemonics to seemingly every object in the house. He replaced notes with a clearer hand than she could produce, but their daughter would not let that sort of life continue. Mom, she said, was getting older, and Dad, you're getting older, too. Melinda was carried to a home in her dotage, passing away shortly thereafter during one of her beloved, bottomless naps. He straightened, let go of the table and his knee. But his steps were sluggish, and the pang of his bladder was joined by pressure against his temples, as if a bubble were expanding inside his head. The force reached his ears and deafened him. He wondered if the person writing his obituary would confuse Cornell Peoples II and Cornell Peoples III. If so, his father might die twice and he would not die once. With their resemblance in face, in name, in profession, he might fool death's registrar and be allowed a return to earth. Any earlier point in his life, he would have laughed at the notion. Cornell was unsure if he was moving—but he was, his pace slow and determined. Then he saw it, finally, as it had to be: the orangish, lukewarm illumination of the bathroom's nightlight.

A Place I Remember

Turning his head partway, Sasha answered, "Right, heat's included but you pay cooking gas," wagging a finger to his side as he spoke while moving upward and forward. His English wore a Serbian overcoat and keys jangled in his left hand, red suspenders creating mortar joints against the flesh of his stout back and attaching to the waistband of stretchy, indigo denim jeans. I watched the heels of his chestnut boots ascend the maroon-carpeted stairs, my right hand, unusual for me, tracing the banister as we spiraled to the second floor. Three knocks against the front door preceded his announcement, "It's Sasha," and we stood briefly as he found the correct key. Twice more he knocked then moved to unlock the door, which opened and prompted him to say, "Ah! you're here, I'm showing the apartment."

"Yeah, the management office told me," she replied, introducing herself as Grace. She was in jeans, too, but of a dark blue and cuffed around her ankles, a white t-shirt, and thick, grey cotton socks that were purple on the toes and heels. "So, this is it."

When Sasha spoke, he at times extended his fingers starting with his thumbs as if objects were being counted. "Like we discussed, one bedroom," he said, displaying a thumb, "living room, a little nook area off the kitchen," now signing an L.

"And it's twelve-fifty a month?" I asked.

"Yes, twelve-fifty."

The living room was decorated with houseplants, two bookshelves of mostly fiction, a television and oval-shaped coffee table, and matching carmine red couch and armchair over which hung five starry lights of an arc lamp. Sunlight permeated through a set of balcony doors. Sasha escorted me through the apartment, but as typically happened, imagining myself and possessions in spaces as I walked from room to room was difficult. The memories of another life, the texture of another history saturated the floor, the walls, the air, and even the imposition of a made-up reality seemed a crime against the existence of another soul. But turning my life into an extension of theirs lessened that disquiet. Grace and I had full-size beds, so mentally replacing hers somehow felt a lesser transgression, and testing the bathroom sink, shower, and toilet joined us in the democracy of bodies. In the kitchen, I ran the sink as well and commented on the amount of counter space.

Sasha told me, "You like the place, I can tell."

"I do, it's really nice," I replied, "I could see myself living here."

"Good, good. It's a quiet neighborhood and I make sure everything in the building is taken care of."

We returned to the living room as Grace watered a dracaena. Putting the can down, she touched her stomach once, softly, as if something lighter than a fetus had kicked her and, with a false smile of embarrassment, said, "Sorry, guys," before opening the balcony doors. I walked toward them, never sensing the uninvited guest, and Grace stepped aside. The balcony was small, perhaps two feet long by five feet wide, just large enough to give a speech to the park it overlooked.

"That's a great spot for people watching all summer," Grace said, "You can get a pretty good view of sunrise, too, if you're up that early."

"All the tenants love that," Sasha added, "Fireworks on the Fourth, lotsa stuff."

Grace said, …

Then Sasha said, …

I was unmoored from their presence, the life in that park engrossing me. It was a simple area with a blacktop and tennis court in one corner and a playground below them, the rest only grass freckled by trees. The voices and barks, the laughter reached me in a lovely discordance then sound by sound fell away until one remained. "Good boy," she was saying, "Good boy," taking a ball from the mouth of a liver and white Brittany. Her dark hair was still worn in a ponytail, the tip of which neared her waist, and she wore turquoise running shorts, her old, tan Birkenstocks with a black tank top that exposed a grey sports bra underneath. From her knees she threw the ball again, the dog catching it after a single bounce.

I could not sleep and was lying in a darkened morning. She was next to me unawakened, the gamboge haze of a security light penetrating the closed blinds. I shifted from my side to back, placed a folded pillow beneath my head. The hours I watched pass, blackness succumbing to a silvery gloam that revealed her bare leg curved above the bedsheets, then ochers and yellows slowly illuminating the room. I lowered my eyelids and imagined the very scene to which I'd blinded myself, a blanketed corner of the mattress, pull chains following the orders of a ceiling fan, her now leaving an unbroken slumber, and kept them closed as replication married reality. Her legs, she stretched them over the bed's port side, and her feet, they bent the hardwood into morning bells. Instead of turning the slats, she drew the blinds with two unapologetic tugs before opening the window completely. Looking into the sunlight, "Bonjour, mon amour," she said then returned to bed by crawling over me. She laid her head on my arm, angled her left leg between mine. I crossed my ankles, braiding our limbs, and responded, *Bon-sure, mon a-moor.* She giggled and positioned herself on an elbow to teasingly pull and hold my jaws and lips as we repeated the phrase. Bonjour, mon amour, bonjour, mon amour, bonjour, mon amour, bonjour, mon amour, bonjour, mon amour. We laid in bed the entire morning: she slept and woke every few minutes, I set out for the kingdom of sleep but never reached its borders.

Turning from the park, "Where's the laundry room?" I asked. Sasha responded, "Right downstairs. I'll show you."

"Wonderful, the building where I am now, it's like walking across a football field to reach it."

I thanked Grace, we wished each other well, and Sasha and I exited the backdoor. Reaching the alley, Sasha flipped through his keys to find the laundry room's, but I told him, "I don't need to see it. I just like to know where it is, but from everything I've seen, I trust this is a really nice building."

"Are you sure?" he replied, pointing a thumb at a mahogany brown door about seven or eight feet away with a dome-shaped security camera above it. "It's no problem."

"That's fine. I liked everything I saw, there's no need to peek at a few washers and dryers."

"Two washers, two dryers," he said, "One dollar to wash and one dollar to dry." I nodded and muttered an affirmatory, "Ah," then Sasha continued, "If you like the place, the application is online and you should complete it as soon as you can. I have another viewing this afternoon and maybe another. We'll see."

"Okay," I responded, smiling, "I've got all that information."

He said, "Nice to meet you, sir," to which I responded, "Same here," and we shook hands.

The park was indecipherable from the other sounds I heard. Roofers were talking in a language I couldn't understand, the unmistakable click of someone coasting on a freewheel bike, somewhere above me air conditioners were running and dripping water onto the pavement. A plane flew overhead and I stopped walking to watch it pass in the opposite direction, too far away to see anything but its white belly and the red and blue stripes on its tailfin. I asked myself, "Does 'je t'aime' still mean 'I love you' in French?" I could also hear my steps restart on the gravel, which were no faster or slower than usual. Reaching the street, I turned away.

Chris

"I was lucky to get his job, I was lucky to get this job," refrains every morning from somewhere in my head as though I need convincing. My eyes open, "I was lucky to get this job, I was lucky to get this job … ," before whispering to my wife, "Good morning, I love you," before turning sideways to leisurely liberate the night's gas, but it's clear to me, as clear as the expression of an underwhelmed lover, that I was very lucky to get his job. Life history is the only persuasion I need. My previous employer was a startup called Excuse Me that matched restaurants with on-call workers. As the company envisioned our future, restaurants were certain to get rid of in-house employees and a step in the transition would be obtaining workers posthaste if one of the hired staff couldn't make it. The pool of eligible workers would first be former and current restaurant employees, but in time it would include the entire population. Think about it, bussing tables and washing dishes are simple tasks, and taking orders nowadays consist of pressing pictured buttons on a screen. The people you need are cooks and bartenders: every waiter, busboy, dishwasher, hostess could be plucked from the street as needed. And this, I thought, was an extremely clever idea. I was an assistant to the head of sales, a young man about half my age and five times my salary. He was a nice boss and given his youth and position of authority, well adjusted, though he kept a mini fridge of Monster Energy in his office and ended conversations by making that sucking sound with his jaw, tongue, and teeth, and saying, "'Kay, 'kay." Nevertheless, this startup exploded during takeoff and I was let go, or "dismissed from further employment" as the company email said. Before that I'd made a career and decent living as a project administrator. The types of projects didn't matter—they could have been learning modules or product launches—and for years I moved from company to company with relative ease and economic security. Very relative, let me add. And before that was the last time I faced life-altering precarity (a tortuous backstory informs this bout with unemployment, but I hope it quenches your curiosity to know it involved taking a stand for myself). This period was also when my first marriage ended. In retrospect, the divorce was about mismatched personalities as much as finances—she loved dancing, for instance, while the custom always struck this atheist as having religious overtones—though a lack of cash never helps when the heart is involved. It's easier to be full of love when your pockets are filled with money. With that bit of history out of the way, I was unemployed and, chastened by that divorce, worried my second wife and I would also split, she and I having made life more complicated by producing two children.

Most people, a group that includes me, would bet against a man in his fifties entering the tech field with no prior experience. I possess no wizardry with code and outright lack my colleagues' youthful enthusiasm for risk-taking. Even for my relatively minor support and administrative roles, you'd expect these shortcomings to eliminate me as a candidate, but they haven't. It's odd and I don't believe in fate, yet not long after Excuse Me's demise, I interviewed twice with Catalogue Corporation, Cat Corp for short. Based on the job listing and its website, I didn't have a good idea of what the company did: a book publisher, perhaps, or a kind of go-between for artists and copyright officials were my guesses, but few things are as inexplicable as how small firms describe themselves. Everything about it was splashy and vague, but I was jobless, and despite my leeriness, I was and remain devoted, undyingly devoted, to keeping my wife and children. (Not a paragraph ago I mentioned this fact, but it's of the utmost importance you know this about me.) The first interview took place over the phone, and my only preparation from

Cat Corp was that it would be with "the team." This information was conveyed via email from an Eve Rudolph, their head of HR, whose look strikingly matched her name. Rudolph was young, like almost everyone but me, and fair-skinned with sheeny black hair tucked into a little bun at the back of her head. Her cheeks and fingernails were red as was the tip of her small and pointed nose. She also wore the first time we met a red blouse with white polka dots. Remember these important details for later as I've gotten ahead of myself by describing her appearance. Preparing as I always have for phone interviews, I rehearsed answers to stock questions and followed a morning routine as if I were going to an office, which included putting on my best suit and tie; with my attaché case on the kitchen table and opened onto copies of my résumé, a legal pad, and ink pens, I was ready come what may when they called at 10:02 and introduced themselves. (We were scheduled for 10:00.) Dan, cofounder and chief technology officer; the senior vice-president of marketing introduced herself as Megan then added, "But call me Meg"; Corey, cofounder and CEO, who added mnemonically that his middle and last names were Edward and Olsen; and Ryan, the executive vice-president of production and person who'd be my boss. Phones are a terrible way to judge someone's character, decide if they're a good workplace fit. In any social gathering, I become a reflector, taking what the person emits and returning it to them. Making yourself a mirror is a well-established tactic for interpersonal success (and succeeding interpersonally is a requisite for succeeding in business which is a requisite for succeeding in life). People are shallow by nature and want to see themselves everywhere: this explains social media and why storefront windows double as looking glasses. Moreover, interviews are already games of guess what's in my pocket, but those over the phone turn the process into games of blindfolded charades. During our conversation, I sometimes confused the voices of Ryan and Meg and often had no idea if the man speaking was Corey or Dan. But I did my best, answering their questions without referring to the interviewees by name:

"Tell us a little about yourself."

"Why'd you apply for the position?"

"How do you see yourself and your skill set evolving with the company?" Etcetera and so forth.

If honesty and frankness were valued, I would have answered, "I'm a frightened and unemployed man, closer to Medicare than puberty," "I need a job," "I hope to become less worried about ending up homeless," but honesty and frankness are valued as ways to describe oneself, not as traits people want in a person. Instead, I told them I was a "straight shooter," the company appeared "on the cusp of something great," "I see myself developing along with the firm's growth and needs, doing whatever's necessary to push us to higher and higher levels of success" (unable to see them, speaking about the firm and myself as an "us" was especially important). Yet, through all their questions and my answers, it was damned hard to know what the company did. Other than "What's your favorite joke?" (to which I answered, "What do you call a dessert you can't put down? A sticky bun."), I could have been interviewing with AT&T or a mom-and-pop restaurant. Then, however, "We've left some time for questions you may have for us. Is there anything you want to know?" With the help of present-day knowledge, it's obvious Ryan was speaking. Her tone is a little dismissive, her words are a skosh too quick, she bookends some of her statements with a breathy "Well" and "See," and moreover, common sense dictates the possible boss ask the prospective direct-report this question. "Yes, thanks, I do have a couple of questions: Could you tell me how you see this position evolving and how you see the company growing and changing over time?" They said nothing worth mentioning about the open gig, but I finally got a description of Cat Corp's business.

Catalogue Corporation was preparing for a post-government world. According to the voice I can now peg as Corey's, within one or two decades, maybe sooner, the task of doling out copyrights and trademarks would be given to business. His case was persuasive: "What's the government's interest in being the record keeper for a Van Moon book? Almost nothing really. If someone infringes a copyright or a trademark, lawyers in the private sector litigate with an appeal to the records that governments keep. But let's say you take the government out of the equation altogether and let the private sector handle it. Also, let's say the private sector develops a way to copyright works instantaneously, like if you self-publish or upload your own music online, and on top of that, establishes a central, worldwide clearing house that anyone anywhere—individuals, companies—can send their material and, for a little fee, have it verified against a massive, real-time updating database and be granted a copyright, a trademark and have it be as quick as paying for something at a store. Governments could get rid of all these massive bureaucracies and implement a small tax on every transaction. It's a win for creators, a win for governments, a win for most everyone." I could hear Ryan, Meg, and Dan smiling as Corey spoke, and I was smiling, too. It sounded genius. Within a year Dan and his people were releasing step one, a technology culling the National Intellectual Property Administration in China, the US Patent and Trademark Office, the European Union Intellectual Property Office, and the Indian Patent Office for to-the-second issuance of trademarks. And I'd gone from having no idea what these people did to imagining an IPO in which I banked millions. The call ended, I pounded my fists on the table, practically screaming, "Oooh, this would be good!" as I imagined this company being the last place I'd work and a family life floating atop the weightless clouds of riches. A fist continued pounding as I stood to put away my things and change into proper unemployed clothes.

In the patch of joblessness before Cat Corp, my days consisted of managing the household for the first time—I cooked, I cleaned, I bought groceries, I did laundry, I ran errands that freed up our nights and weekends—which had the peculiar effect of briefly erasing from our memories how we survived when my wife, Donna, and I both had full-time positions. But we remembered and relearned soon after I restarted being paid for my labor and have since been hurried and in need of more time. Another oddity, this also unexpected, was not just the pride I took in handling my tasks, completing them even if the result was merely good enough, but the unspoken self-assuredness about my place in the family. It's a little vainglorious to look around and notice your imprint everywhere, to also know your caprice is the difference between order and confusion, but this control is what I felt. (One can't give that power up without some reluctance, but we needed another income and my preference has always been non-domestic work.) That sense of potency linked up with post-interview excitement following the call, and I rushed, gamboled perhaps, through my chores—sweeping with the hurried back-and-forth motion of an indecisive mind and scrubbing the bathroom tile as though it were splattered with some luckless first date's blood. Nor did driving our wine-red second car, blotched with bird poop and greened with pollen, to the supermarket lessen my enthusiasm, which admittedly, was premature. I'd obviously not received follow-up from Cat Corp within hours of the interview—in fact, Corey said I would "hear something in about a week"—and with retrospect, how I felt about my performance was an effect of how much I wanted the job. Desperation plus opportunity plus desire is the equation for hope or delusion. But I'm not a head of state, just an average man, middle-class in everything from manners to capital, so any downsides of overconfidence are confined to myself and family—pity them and me for that.

One of the duties of my joblessness was having food available for the kids' after-school snacks. (For the sake of family time, but mostly to indicate our lives would be okay, I once picked them up, wanting to go for ice cream sundaes, but they opened the doors of our hatchback like blackmail victims and sat, one in front and the other in back, silently looking out the rolled-down windows as if they planned to escape at a red light. I was certain they needed reassurance—and I'd spent much of the day fantasizing about scoops of vanilla bean ice cream and a crisp, sweet waffle cone succumbing to my bite—but a harmless joke I made to comfort them and salvage the afternoon did neither. I looked over my shoulder at little Samuel and, returning my eyes to the street, met the face of Eleanor then said, feigning some anger, "Sad looking … We may have to get used to being in this car if something doesn't change soon." Not since he was a small child had Samuel cried that uncontrollably, emitting a wordless and teary shriek like those news cameras capture of family members at a murder scene. Eleanor cried, too, but also turned away from me with such violence I initially thought she was throwing herself out the window. Maybe the idea occurred to her and she withstood the command. That answer I will never know, but thereafter we went home, where I also failed at convincing them not to tell their mother.) Our kids are not hard to please, for which I'm grateful, so having some type of not-too-bad junk food sufficed. The day of my phone interview I wanted to meet them at the door—another sign of excitement was placing those bite-size pizzas in the oven later than I should have—but instead of greeting their entrance with food, I was sliding the little morsels onto plates with a spatula when they came into the kitchen.

"Why are you smiling?" Eleanor, the oldest, asked.

Samuel followed, "I'm hungry."

They resemble each other more than they resemble their parents. Eleanor and Samuel's ears are semicircles with almost no lobes and rise just a little from their heads as if shyness keeps them from protruding. I've wondered if this feature was atavistic, but I can recall no one in my family with ears like theirs and Donna's knowledge of her family doesn't go back more than one generation (I will never understand her contentment about that). My children also share a mouth, a pair of thin lips with perfect, straight teeth. Samuel's eyes are a lighter shade, tobacco brown, but their noses are round in the same way—short bridges and nostrils as cute as a stuffed koala's—as are their ovate and tender faces, their gangling physiques. Eleanor and Samuel were twelve and ten, but people believed they were twins. What I found remarkable, however, was that after their births I couldn't remember how I imagined they would look. Before

Eleanor and Samuel were born, I certainly pictured them in my head, and not just ideas of parental amalgams but unique and bodied children, yet my real son and daughter permanently escorted those people away from me. It was as if those prenatal visions had not existed. That's when I first noticed the odd phenomenon of real-life effacing someone's fantasized appearance.

"Am I smiling?" I answered.

"Yes, a lot," she said, "I've never seen you smile that much."

Samuel repeated, "A lot," then spat onto his plate some food that was too hot. "That's disgusting," his sister interjected as he took the moist and mangled, tooth-marked clump into his palms, blew on it, and made a second, successful attempt eating. "So gross," she added and turned to me for an answer.

"Well, I had a really good interview today, that's all," I replied, "And I've been excited about it."

With genuine enthusiasm, "That's awesome," said Eleanor who, learning from Samuel's experience, pushed a stream of air through pursed lips before taking a bite of her snack. "Do you think you'll get it?"

"We shall see. Today was just the first interview, over the phone, and I should hear back from them within a week about coming in for a face to face. But our talk went really well."

"Oh," Eleanor responded, "That's good, too. I'm happy for you." She had, I know, expected more. She wanted me to say the job was at hand. She wanted to feel our insecurity recede. But I gave them something less than a promise, something even less than hope. What had I offered them actually, smiling and upbeat as I was, other than perhaps a chance to believe life could also change for the good at any moment? If clinging to that was enough to fortify me, it had to be enough for them.

"I'm happy for you, too, Dad," Samuel added.

By the time Donna returned, my confidence was tempered and competing with disquiet. Eleanor's reaction along with my rerunning of the interview, trying to recall what was said and how it was uttered, had changed my outlook. But I'd promised myself well before I knew of Cat Corp's existence that I would no longer show doubt: sadness, uncertainty, stress, every negative and unhelpful expression needed to be masked. These emotions we all felt, but it was most harmful if I, more than anyone else, released that noxious substance into our air. So when Donna saw me, I immediately smiled and asked about her day. Rolling her head back, Donna shoveled hair from her face with a crescent-shaped hand. Her hair is black and her eyes are an unexceptional brown, but that face and its sarcous cheeks and lips and dimpled chin, touched by an intimation of makeup, is prettier than any I will ever see. She answered, setting her messenger bag on the floor, where it teetered and collapsed as if its blood pressure had fallen. She removed her shoes, an indigo pair with tiny heels, and lay back on the couch, feet angled inwards and the curve of a bent arm resting atop her forehead. Never an easy day when you're the sole earner, even with a husband doing what he can—ordering the household, tweaking and sending his résumé to any passable job opening. Seeing her, I wished there was more I could do besides providing the same less than hope I'd given my children. Donna straightened her legs, sat up, put her arm down, "Just tired," she said and yawned. "Do you remember that kid I told you about, Cameron, who's always bouncing off the walls?"

"ADHD?"

"Well, yes. Everyone believes he has ADHD except his parents. He was drawing on his legs today, with an ink pen, no less. These kind of weird, kind of interesting flower petal-looking shapes."

Before I could utter something supportive, Donna yawned into cupped hands and asked, "How were things today?"

"I had that phone interview this morning," I replied, to which she grinned and leaned onto her knees, "It went well. About a week is the time frame they gave for possible next steps."

"Wonderful!" she responded. Perhaps it's a trait of someone my age but a fatigued and happy woman, regardless of why, is one of the most erotic scenes you can witness—promise and vulnerability emanating from the curves and lines of Donna's face incites hedonism in me. I would have made love to her that instant if Sam and Eleanor hadn't been loose in the house.

Three days later an email from Rudolph invited me for an in-person interview to which I again wore my best suit. And meeting her, whatever details of Eve Rudolph's face I'd seen in my head were obliterated: her presence was the perfect crime—killing the imposter, destroying their body, rubbing out incriminating footmarks and fingerprints. No versions of Eve Rudolph existed other than the one standing before me. And the same occurred after she led me through Cat Corp's offices to my four-person interrogation. Composed of book covers, an everchanging, computer-generated, wall-sized picture mosaic was in the lobby, creating a sharpened pencil on the day of my interview, and the floor had reddish-purple carpeting that in the main area became Persian blue. This was a large room with a coffee bar in one corner, around which loveseats were situated. In another section was a digital dartboard and a shuffleboard table. The rest was long desks and computers, some with two monitors, and similar-looking young people that only time would allow me to distinguish. Down a hallway were offices and small glass-paneled conferences rooms, to one of which Rudolph opened a door, revealing Dan, Corey, Meg, and Ryan sitting around a hexagon-shaped table (whether by intent or not, Rudolph pointing to and describing knickknacks on our path kept me from noticing the four of them until we entered). They stood to introduce themselves as Rudolph backed out of the room, shutting the door with the emotionless smile of a person who's waited too long for a picture to be taken, and once more, any ideas of how the quartet would appear evaporated when I saw how they did. The geometry of Dan's trimmed beard is the obvious work of a high-end salon, and as I would find out, he belongs to the species of man that wears a fashionable tie with nice shirts but never suits; Meg is a blonde of about average height with a full-figured amount of flesh on her bones (though I understand the rules governing flattery nowadays are fluid, people of my generation and older recognize this as a compliment); Corey's shaved head is the obvious result of making lemonade out of male-pattern-baldness lemons and his style is long-sleeved shirts with undone cuffs, flapping like birdlets of busyness; Ryan's dark bronze-dyed hair is low along the sides and curly on top while her eyes are a flickering light green that give the impression she's high.

With our work-or-starve world, in-person interviews are the sole defensible way for hiring—meeting people who decide your fate at least provides the arrangement a touch of morality. One must see the despair in your eyes and hear the need in your voice before sentencing you to further privation. That said, I dislike the multi-person, parole-board types of interviews: turning from one person to another, duplicating an interviewer's affect and mannerisms as you answer is more difficult than the questioners know, particularly if it's done well. But a positive of being older and having lived through spells of unemployment is my experience in these settings—if interviewing was my job, I'd be an accomplished and wealthy man—which is why I succeeded with Dan, Corey, Ryan, and Meg. Their smiles and laughter, though not good indications with every hirer, fed my performance, and I became looser, of course smiling and laughing, even taking the chance at self-deprecation (typically unwise for interviewees). "My cellphone is with me at all times," I said, "just in case there're no payphones." Another instance, "That 'twit' in Twitter must be for me, because I don't understand any of it." The position, as I understood it, was also straightforward research and data entry—combing public repositories for trademarks and copyrights to test and load into Cat Corp's database. "Anyone can do that, but hell, I'm the person who's here," I thought, "This job is mine to lose." Rarely have I been as confident as I was leaving Cat Corp's offices that morning, with a second assurance of hearing from them in about a week. On my way home I stopped for two freshly baked, moist-to-the-touch glazed doughnuts from a local Krispy Kreme (with Eleanor and Samuel at school and Donna at work, it wasn't a sin to buy a treat just for me). Again the children came home and noticed my excitement, which I refused to hide from Donna when she arrived and couldn't have if I wanted. No part of me feared setting them or myself up for disappointment, and less than a week later, I was proven right.

I arrived the first day overdressed—slacks a professional shade of midnight blue, black dress shoes, starched white shirt, and combining the main colors, a black-and-blue-striped necktie—which I imagine was unsurprising to my coworkers, any of whom could have been my child had I started fatherhood earlier in life. After greetings with the foursome, Ryan gave an overview of the work and introduced my colleagues. Three of us were involved with the "search and rescue mission," as our task was nicknamed. Rob is thin and keeps his blond hair tapered along the sides and high on top, like a bit of well-formed toothpaste squeezed from the tube, he wears t-shirts most days and alternates between an ill-formed chin beard and a meticulously square soul patch. My seat is at the end of a rectangular table and Rob sits to my right. Across from me is Eddie, the name I use if he's not around because he prefers Edward. The frames of his glasses are round and large, and the features of his face are normal. His eyes are a deep, dark brown, indeed almost black, which beneath the lenses can give the impression he's underwater, but I wouldn't say this is weird, just a statement of fact. Eddie's lips are smaller than standard, like a hyphen separating two words, but also nothing out of the ordinary, yet he does maintain a high-top fade that feels out of place for someone who seems otherwise uninterested in devoting time to personal grooming. He's not disheveled, granted, rather a utilitarian who chooses outfits with coordinating colors and avoiding wrinkles in mind and not stylishness. On that first Monday, I could not have predicted becoming fixated on him, coming to note the details of character that made Eddie Eddie as opposed to Rob or Corey or Samuel—such as the way he placed a hand on his cheek for a moment of thought before returning it to his desk—matching his fixation with me or, more correctly, his fixation with Chris. It was that Monday when he first looked across the table and called me "Chris," in fact, waiting three or four seconds before shaking his head as if he were destroying an old memory or jump-starting the formation of a new one then using my name.

I thought it a mistake, and for an extremely long period, this was the benefit of doubt I gave though I didn't know who Chris was or why Eddie confused me with him. Not long after I started, for instance, he and I conversed in the breakroom, a back and forth that started when Eddie said, "Hi, Chris, how's everything going so far, getting the hang of it?" and I, sillily, foolishly, out of some inexplicable reluctance to defend myself or correct someone, answered as though he'd said my birth name: "No complaints, it's been smooth sailing as the old saying goes. You and Rob, everyone actually, have been extremely helpful." Much of this was true. My experience at Cat Corp was going well (tediousness of searching databases and completing spreadsheets, notwithstanding), and my colleagues had been helpful, Eddie included, except for his misnaming tic. Regardless, we talked about fifteen minutes, during which Eddie revealed he was twenty-five years old and Cat Corp was his first "real" job, and he also couldn't figure out the company's business before he was hired. Eddie, moreover, had been with the firm almost a year and didn't anticipate soon looking for another position. "There hasn't been much turnover," he said, "The people are nice and I like the work … I haven't been here long, but it's a place where people enjoy working and want to be." He was young and financially desperate—I remember youth and knew financial desperation—so I took the last part of his statement, re: Cat Corp as a place people want to be, with a proper amount of skepticism. I was happy for my job, too, and still daydreaming of selling my stock (when we received it) and retiring to a country of eternal summer, but no one enjoys work. That's a lie told by charlatans and believed by fools.

Regardless of our age differences, rapport was developed with my colleagues and I did my part by playing the role of old man, joking, as I did during my in-person interview, about technology and how the world had changed since my youth. No arrangement is perfect, but our collegiality rescued us from the unending task we'd been assigned—every day, it seemed, we needed to find and record additional pieces of information—but for me, when the atmosphere wasn't undermined by expecting to hear "Chris," it was ruptured by Eddie actually calling me this name. And it never appeared to be a joke. Each "Chris" was said as though it were an honest misunderstanding, nor did anyone else react with snickers or giveaways that, perhaps, it was part of an odd initiation ritual. Many people, Donna on occasion, too, mistake my nonconfrontational nature with an unwillingness to fight. It's not that but recognition most clashes aren't worth the trouble and neither is possible escalation: wise is my description for avoiding situations in which you say regrettable things or become the victim of regrettable acts. Nevertheless, all people reach a point when they need to speak, and I, one afternoon, corrected Eddie face to face. He shook his head, apologized and used my name, then continued looking at me a few seconds before leaving his chair. I wondered if and when Eddie next appeared he'd be thrusting a knife into my back, but he returned and we didn't speak the remainder of the day. When, however, we next talked, he called me "Chris." It was an embarrassment and, for this reason, I didn't want to tell another person. I went some time having regular meetings with Ryan without mentioning a thing, nor did I give Donna and the children a reason to suspect my troubles. I tried again, in fact, to correct Eddie when Rob asked if anyone was having issues with the internet connection. "I'm not, seems to be working fine with me," Eddie replied, "Chris, what about you?" What about me? The you he spoke to was not the me I am, so I corrected Eddie, and he again responded with a head shake and apology. When I wasn't near him, Eddie's nonsense continued to rattle me, caused me to ask why names had any meaning, why "Chris" wasn't as legitimate a name for me as my own. Furthermore, was he calling me "Chris" or "Kris" or "Criss" or "Khris" or "Cris?" The spelling mattered: I imagined this mistaken-for-me person differently based on the arrangement and appearance of letters. (You have the benefit of knowing what I had to find out.)

"This kid at work, Eddie, must be something wrong with him. He has me … ," I said, my hands strangling an invisible neck.

Donna responded, "What are you talking about?"

Left arm bowed skyward, pit lathered with shaving cream, she made the first downstroke then held the razor beneath a stream of water, sending miniature hairs down the drain as I watched. Donna did not dance and allowed me this harmless perversity, irrefutable signs of a soulmate.

"Eddie, the person who sits across from me," I told her, "You won't believe this, but he keeps calling me 'Chris,' as if it's my name. He says it then shakes his head, like 'Oops, made that mistake again.'"

"I don't understand, he calls you another name, then what, you answer?"

Before responding, I collected myself to stifle the willies in my stomach. My fear was Eddie's issue—and it was Eddie's issue— would be interpreted as my failing, that a wrong I suffered was due to an action I had not taken. People wish to believe in their control of events. But I did not found Cat Corp or hire myself or Eddie, to recite just three necessary parts of this matter. Donna was removing the final hairs at the tip-top of that diamond-shaped dimple and peeked at me for a reply.

"That's it, I've corrected him, and he keeps doing it. There's no way he doesn't know my name. But the mistake, if you want to call it that, seems earnest."

"What does he do when you correct him?"

"Apologize, I said."

"You didn't say he apologizes."

Not with palmfuls of water but fingers dampened by a spurt from the faucet, Donna washed her armpit before drying it with a towel and applying aftershave lotion. She bowed her right arm, wet her fingers in a cool rivulet, then lathered that precious hollow with shaving cream.

"Well, he apologizes and does it again. The next day or day after, I don't think he's ever said my name. Has he? … No, I don't believe so. There has to be something wrong with him, right?"

"Yes, he sounds cuckoo. But regardless, that's harassment and you shouldn't sit there and take it," she replied, "You should tell him to cut it out and go to your supervisor if he doesn't." Pausing mid-downstroke, Donna turned to me, arm still positioned as though she planned to elbow me across the face or invite my lips to her comely and frothy cove. (It was neither: Donna loathed violence, having once compelled me to buy mousetraps that didn't kill the rodents, and though she permitted the voyeuristic pleasure of looking, she detested the feel of lips on her underarms.) "If he does it again, do something. Otherwise, he'll be harassing you as long as you're there or force you to quit, which cannot happen. Not right now."

"You're right," I answered, waiting until she'd finished shaving the last irresistible indent to leave. "I'll have to speak with Ryan if he doesn't cut it out."

Before I left the house for an evening walk, I stopped to look at a family photo. It was a couple of years old and taken at a department store with a background of skyline blue that faded into cloudlike white at the top of the frame. Samuel and I had dressed in red neckties, blue shirts, and khaki slacks, and Donna and Eleanor wore tea rose sundresses with flower patterns—Eleanor sitting on my lap, Samuel sitting on Donna's. That afternoon Samuel was fussy and refused to smile. Promising a new toy (which also required promising the same for Eleanor) persuaded him to comply, however, and it took weeks before they forgave our reneging on that vow. This picture was hanging near the front door, and as I eyed it and remembered that day and many others, I realized Eleanor and Samuel were in the room behind me. He was sitting on the floor, using the living room couch as back support and watching television on an iPad while Eleanor paced back and forth, as she often did, while concentrating on her phone. Not a power on earth would separate me and my children.

The following day I went to Ryan's office when I arrived—waiting for Eddie's next hostile act was not an option. To my knock she responded, "Good morning, I didn't know we were scheduled to meet today," which may have been harmless but sounded to me as though I were being accused of interrupting.

"We're not but I needed to speak with you."

"Well, of course, what's up?"

I sat and briefly touched my cheek, before letting my hand dangle over the edge of the chair's armrest. "I've been having this issue with Eddie—Edward. He doesn't say my name. Whenever he speaks to me, he calls me 'Chris.' I initially thought it was an accident, at some point I corrected him, but he doesn't stop. It's weird and frustrates me. I have a name that's mine, but for some reason, he refuses to use it. And it's not, or doesn't seem to be, a joke with him. It's, I don't know, I don't understand."

As I spoke, Ryan tilted her head a little sideways as though the motion enhanced her ability to understand. "That … is … weird. Does he mention a last name?"

Her question caused me to wonder if he'd done this before and a particular surname was the corroboration she needed. "No," I answered, "never has that I can remember."

"Well, okay, I ask because someone named Chris used to sit where you are now, Chris Steen. Maybe that has something to do with it," Ryan said, lowering one eyebrow and lifting the other, "They started around the same time. This is total conjecture that him calling you Chris and Chris Steen are related. I'm trying to make sense of what's happening in real-time, see."

"Chris Steen," I repeated, bringing to mind an image of this person that was inseparable from my appearance.

"Yeah, you stepped into his role. This has been going on since you started?"

"The entire time, I don't think he's used my name once. Not once."

"Okay, wow," Ryan said, "I will talk with Edward and get back with you. Does that work?"

"Sure, that's fine with me. Thank you so much."

"No problem, thank you for finally bringing this to my attention. I'll get to the bottom of this, very strange … "

That Ryan said I'd "finally" told her registered, but I chose not to let that characterization bother me. Her promise to speak with Eddie was an achievement—this I could tell myself and Donna—yet whether or not he was fixable, she'd given me a clue. Unearthing Chris Steen's existence was critical, most importantly how he looked, and doing so was all I thought about when I reached my desk. But with my computer monitor visible to everyone, I had to settle for anticipation until I returned home, not wanting people to notice a series of multiracial headshots on my screen and gossip about what the hell I was doing. Meanwhile, whenever Eddie left his desk, I assumed it was to meet with Ryan even though his manner revealed nothing when he came back. He was, to my exasperation, a white wall of demeanor. Regardless, Eddie left that evening with a "Have a nice day," and after a "Thanks, and to you as well," I was behind him moments later, which for a second felt as though I were trailing him until we reached the parking lot and diverged to our cars.

I made it home before Donna, and fortunate boy was I, Eleanor and Samuel were busying themselves with matters they pretended to be homework. Without undressing or removing my shoes, I went to our shared office and opened thousands of window tabs, figuratively speaking, each with search results for versions of "Chris Steen"— "Kris Steen," "Khris Steen," "Cris Steen," "Krys Steen," "Khrys Steen," "Christopher Steen," "Khristopher Steen," and to cover the remotest possibilities, "Kristoff Steen"—along with "Cat Corp" or "Catalogue Corporation." Much of this was unnecessary, and had I not begun searches before reading the previous results, it would have been obvious that "Chris Steen Catalogue Corporation" yielded the right person. "What a goofy face," I thought before saying aloud,

"He doesn't look anything like me. Not even a young me!" Most of what I discovered about him didn't have to be pieced together: everything was nicely collected in his LinkedIn profile. Assuming he finished high school and college at eighteen and twenty-two, thereabout, Chris was around the same age as Eddie, and confirming what Ryan told me, they'd started at Cat Corp within a month of one another a year ago. The suburban high school he attended was better than average though not elite, which is also how I'd describe his out-of-state college. He was a general studies major and fraternity member, American Red Cross volunteer, and now a media relations coordinator at an environmental group. But to Chris's appearance: his haircut resembles a bob, with bangs lying across his thick eyebrows, the two of which flirted in the center of his forehead. His eyes are small, and based on my squinting at the headshot, brown (those color eyes the lone trait we share), and his nose and bizarrely parted lips are like an arrow pointing downward at a doorbell button. To say I stared at his picture is not an overstatement. Seeing this man's face, I sought a clue that would give Eddie's behavior sense, yet surveying and reflecting, I resolved: bitchy, unapologetic taunting, ignorance and madness, no other reasons materialized.

Donna opening the door mercifully yanked me from the grasp of Eddie and Chris. When she reached me, I put an arm around her waist, "This is the guy I replaced," and she leaned toward the computer.

"Chris Steen," she muttered.

"Yeah, he's the Chris who Eddie apparently believes I resemble. And, you won't believe this, my desk is where he used to sit."

"You don't look a thing like him," Donna continued, "I mean, not even a little." Running a hand down the center of her hair, she added, "I hope you speak with your supervisor."

"I did!" was my riposte, upset she assumed I hadn't and proud because I had, "That's how I know who Chris Steen is, Ryan told me and said she'd speak with Eddie then get back with me."

She drew my head into her body as a hug, "Okay, things

should hopefully be taken care of. Maybe Eddie just needs a pair of glasses or—"

"He does wear glasses!"

"Sor-ry. I must have forgotten," replied an agitated Donna, "or he's just nuts."

Near the top of my inbox the next morning was a request from Ryan that I see her when I arrived. Reaching her office, "Is now fine?" I asked.

"Definitely, come in, let me call Corey. He's coming, too."

I thought my life was over in a very literal sense of the cliché: They were going to fire me—Why else did the CEO need to be present?—and when it happened, Donna would leave and take the kids. A man in his fifties, often unemployed with little prospect for changing that reality, divorcing him is more rational than a dropped baseball hitting the grass. For me there would not be a new beginning. Life without Donna and my children is not a life worth living; I am not, could never be, a weekends and holidays father. Separation would be the coda to my existence. Ryan asked how I was doing, and I tried to control my breathing as I spoke. Her demeanor was unchanged because executions are only unusual to the executed. Seconds later Corey entered and shut the door, angled his seat toward me in a fashion that gave the impression he and I were equals.

"Should I start … ?" Ryan directed at Corey.

He responded, "Sure, I'll jump in as needed."

"Well, yesterday we, Corey and I, spoke with Edward, and we wanted to tell you that he'll be taking a leave of absence." Corey looked at me then turned his eyes to Ryan without moving his head. "We can't get too much into the details of our conversation obviously, but what you can know is that he was having an issue of sorts. A personal, emotional thing, if you understand what I'm saying." I understood the words she was using but not their meanings. They were a chain of syllables, which when placed together were recognizable but incomprehensible. Yet I nevertheless told her what she said was understood, stipulating "so far." She continued, "You should know also that Edward didn't have a beef with you. It's an issue he has to deal with. And let me add, too, because this is important: we don't believe he's a threat to you in any way. If we thought differently, he would've been terminated and ordered not to come back. We are very firm on employee safety, having a violence-free workplace, see."

For this assurance, Corey and Ryan might have expected my gratitude. Instead, I ignored that unenforceable safety guarantee and tried to get more details from them about Eddie. "Could you tell me a little about what was going on? That much involves me," I responded, "I'm the reason, if you want to look at it that way, he's taking a leave and isn't here."

She looked to Corey who had placed his elbows on his stomach and a right fist into a palm, sending his shirt cuffs to the middle of his forearms, then sucked in a nasally breath. "Totally fair. I'll try to say as much as I can without divulging Edward's personal matters. To put it, well, let me say it this way: Edward was having a difficult time adjusting to Chris leaving. Um, it's complicated, but the, in his words, 'routine' and 'comfort' of having Chris as his coworker was lost."

"Were they close?" I asked.

"Not particularly from what I could glean," Corey answered, looking to Ryan.

She concurred, "From what I gather, they were not close. Just coworkers based on my understanding."

"I don't understand."

Corey maneuvered into a leg-over-leg cross, flashed a smile of bewilderment, "That could be said about us, too. The best way to explain it, based on my understanding, is Edward was used, very used to seeing Chris sitting across from him every day. I guess, something was comforting about that, so when Chris left, he experienced a loss there, even though the two of them weren't close. It …"

"Yeah, apparently," Ryan interjected, "he would see you in the morning and think you didn't belong, that something was off, and calling you 'Chris' was his obviously poor way of handling the situation."

"But as Ryan stated we don't believe he's a threat to you," Corey said, "This is an emotional, mental health issue, something we think can be handled with time away and some counseling resources, which we've directed him to utilize. I'll also add that we don't know how long Edward will be out, but a few weeks at least is our guess. Again, though, we can't speak to any of his personal health information or any other types of private details."

What I hadn't expected from myself was pity for Eddie, but intermingled with confusion about what they told me and rage at being his target was sympathy for him. I had never heard of such a pathetic and baffling reaction to a coworker quitting. Just imagine how Eddie would react to serious hurt, a loved one dying or a partner walking away, rather than a person who is, in effect, a stranger leaving for greener pastures. And the pitiful bastard took his misplaced feelings out on me. When our talk about Eddie concluded, Corey left the room, saying, "I believe there's something Ryan needs to speak with you about, but if you have any questions, any issues whatsoever about anything whatsoever, know you can come to us about it."

"Well, relatedly but also a little change of direction," Ryan started, "Before we launch our technology—the work you, Rob, and previously Edward were working on, which has been great by the way—we've decided to expand its scope before introducing it. What that means is along with cataloguing trademarks and copyrights, we will also catalogue every book that's been published in the past and that is being published currently in real-time, see," and she beamed as if she'd flung on the lights at a surprise birthday party.

"Which would entail the same work we're doing now," I responded.

"Yes, it does but with a couple of add-ons or additions. Well, you will also be searching the Amazon and Barnes and Nobles websites for books, just going through what they're selling, so major publishers, small publishers, self-published books, and matching that with information from government sources. We didn't expect this step to happen now—it was always planned for the future, but in considering it more, Corey, Dan, Meg, and I came to the opinion this was vital in order for us to hit the ground running when we go public, see."

That's when I smiled, "There will be stock options then, for those of us who work here."

She again turned her head as though I were *Blue Poles*, and I continued, "You said 'when we go public,' I figured that meant go public as in an IPO."

"Oh, I see what you're saying. We're not there yet. I meant 'go public' as in releasing our technology. Not saying that won't happen, just it isn't what I was referring to."

"Makes sense, that's probably still a ways off."

"Yes, that's right. One more thing before you leave: I know you, Rob, and Edward had divvied up the work in a really effective manner, but we won't be able to bring in a replacement while Edward is out. Particularly without knowing how long his absence will be, it didn't make a lot of sense organizationally—taking time from you and Rob to train a contractor, who may not be here for long, all while ramping up this new feature."

"I understand, it's better to have us going full speed."

Now you understand my predicament. That meeting happened a month ago and I've no clue if or when Eddie will return, and assuming he does, whether I'll become Chris again. Yet that may be preferable to the last four weeks. Having more work and being one man down, Rob and I are busier than either of us could've envisioned when we accepted jobs at Cat Corp. I come to the office bearing a tiredness that's only a tad ameliorated from the previous day: work tacks on interest that outstrips my sleep payments. What energy remains I try to use being a decent husband and father, which must suffice. I cannot quit, and honestly, if it were possible, I wouldn't want to—my confidence in this company's ultimate success is unchanged and absolute. Nothing worthwhile is gained without sacrifice and hardship. I quite like that idea, it's intensely quotable. Perhaps, after we receive our shares and those become worth millions, I'll write an you-can-do-it-too book and this will be the epigraph.

The Man Who Loved My Dog

He's standing in the corner of my eye before I hear her speak. When I turn, they scoot backward and she raises a hand to shield her eyes from the sun. Her mask is red plaid and hand-sewn and she pulls it down with the caution of a child unpeeling a bandage to look at a wound. Her teeth are large—wispy, black hairs above her narrow lips—and she asks me, "What happened?" His face is covered with an orange neck gaiter and he's wearing a W baseball cap: its snugness to his head, faded blue, deformed brim are confessions of baldness. They retake each other's hands. Murphy stands, her head bobs curiously, then she sits again on the pavement. Practically shouting through my mask, I answer, "That car was coming down Damen and tried to turn at … " but can't remember the intersection. I look up, continuing before I find the sign, " Argyle, but they didn't see the guy in the bike lane. They smashed right into him." What I do not say is just before the accident my attention was elsewhere. I saw the car approach and the cyclist overpowering his bicycle, but my eyes and head moved away. The cyclist yelled, "Hey!" louder, "Hey!" which is when I looked. Tires screeched, car and bike collided. His body levitated as though he were an action hero front-flipping off his bike, but his feet stopped midair and he thudded chest-and-shoulder first onto the hood of the car.

Raising a hand to her masked face, "Oh, God, I hope everything's alright."

"I think so. He sat on the car for a while, but hopped up. I haven't seen an ambulance either." Murphy stands and looks at me, tugs forward a little, but I don't move. The man and I make eye contact before he gazes at Murphy.

"What breed is she? She?"

"Yeah, she. I don't know for sure. She's mixed with some kind of hound though."

"How old?"

"Two and a half."

"Really pretty dog."

"Thanks." I can tell beneath his face covering is a smile. But she turns to leave, tugging his hand so he would follow, and they walk away without saying anything more. Murphy sits again and the man looks over his shoulder at her.

After the accident, the bicyclist had been moaning and swearing. His left arm was bent in any imaginary sling and he held it around the triceps as he cursed. The driver had jumped out of her car, wailing and clutching her face with both hands. Had she killed him, I believe she might have ripped the skin from her cheeks and forehead. But that scene changed. The bike rider calmed down and started flexing his arm and gesturing, from what I could tell, "I'm fine." The driver's sobs outlasted his assurances, but she calmed, too. More passersby than needed stopped to help. They embraced the cyclist and driver, patted their backs, and eventually, it appeared to me, started having a conversation. Someone actually closed the driver's door, which had been left open when she got out. Murphy stands and tugs harder than she had previously, and I realize she has been standing up and sitting down with each change of the walk sign.

We cross the street, angling away from the impromptu gathering of strangers, head a little north, pass an unused baseball field, then enter near the parking lot. Here I extend her leash and she trots further in front of me. Her coat is tan but she has a touch of white around her nose and her tail curves into a question mark. Watching Murphy roam and sniff Winnemac Park makes me happy—the sort of happiness you experience when someone you love does something that makes them happy. Occasionally, I ask myself if Murphy ever feels she does more for me than I do for her. Any normal, caring person must sometimes wonder, "Am I doing enough?" But, I suppose, in all relationships you trust everything's OK until you can't believe otherwise. That Murphy doesn't respond in the language of humans is also perfect: I have relied, throughout my life, on the substance of actions rather than the promise of words, and on our walks, she often looks back as if to say, "Follow me" or "Let me show you something." Murphy tells me more than she could ever say with speech. We follow a squiggly, concrete, east-west walkway. To both sides of us are native prairie habitats. On our right, tennis courts and a high school football stadium, and farther north, a playground, another football field, baseball fields, and acres of parkland. More diamonds, more parkland, and another playground are to our left. At the park's northeast and northwest corners are massive, prewar era schools, completing my middle-class existence. When we reach Leavitt Street, Murphy and I turn around and head north. That couple is talking, approaching from the other direction: he backhands the air, emphasizing some point, and getting closer, habit bends our paths away from each other. But he notices us and pauses—I know he pauses even though it's an itty-bitty motion—and glances at Murphy as we pass. Murphy is kind with other dogs but mostly a loner. She explores the park, stops here, pisses, kicks up grass, she defecates someplace and I pick it up and toss the baggie in a trash bin. I always do, even when I would rather not because it's too cold or snowy or rainy outside or because her shit is too wet or too smelly. Besides, I am not an intimidating man—not in appearance, not in demeanor. Murphy's obedience is largely due to her goodwill and most people assume I'm a pushover. A good description of myself would be: I look like a man with an imposing friend. If I were to leave her poop in the grass, someone would confront me or, also possible, beat me into compliance. We reach Foster Avenue, the park's northern border, and stroll alongside a fence before circling to where we started.

Our pathway out, on this day at least, slopes a little downhill. A young woman is walking toward us cradling a whitish-brown

Scottish Terrier. She looks into its face and (I imagine) lovingly clucks her tongue, but when Murphy and I are close enough, her head snaps at me as though I pushed open the door to a private room. She looks too quickly for me to turn away, however, so I smile and nod forgetting much of my face is hidden. We sidestep, moving to the pavement's edge: her dog barks and Murphy stops to stare at him, she quiets her dog, but I stop, too. I feel someone behind me and turn my head. That couple steps in the grass to go around us, but he doesn't acknowledge Murphy: they continue talking and he keeps making that backhand motion and I wait to let them walk ahead of us much farther than necessary.

This stranger's hands are flailing—his waving is hyperactive and two-fisted. He is also leaning forward with knees apart welcoming Murphy to come over. Without looking at him, I see his movements. A few seconds pass with him as a lunatic blur in my side vision. My practice is tuning out strangers unless they march into my path. Even shoving flyers into my hand does not slow me. Most people want donations or petition signatures, but if they can be avoided, I keep my eyes in whatever direction I need to dodge them. I especially do not stop for strangers on park benches wordlessly trying to get my dog's attention. Particularly this year: not engaging is common sense. Then, however, in the same motion, I acknowledge this person and Murphy walks to him. The idea of reining her in happens but is not heeded, and she looks up at him as he pets her head and back. His mask is baby blue and tucked under his straight, pointy nose. His pants are dark green and rise too high above his ankles. I can't tell if his white t-shirt is old and washed-out or was purchased that way. But his clothing aside, he is fixated and petting Murphy as if they've been reunited, murmuring "Good dog" and "You're so cute." I wonder if he knows I'm here, if he saw me as Murphy and I approached. I'm standing close enough to be noticed, and of course, a leash runs from her neck to my hand. When I pat my leg and say, "Come on," he finally sees me. He is a young-looking man, though

I guess about thirty years old, with large, springy black curls, and he speaks with his left eyebrow raised a little higher than the other.

"Sorry, I love dogs," he says, rubbing her head, "and this one is beautiful."

"No problem, that's … totally fine. Come on."

"What's her name?"

"Murphy."

"Murphy. Murphy's a famous name."

I pat my leg again but don't give her a command. He is no longer petting as excitedly as he had but is now slowly stroking Murphy from the top of her head to the tip of her tail. "Really? Guess I've never thought about it. That was her name when I got her, but the only famous one I can think of is Edie."

He smiles, "Eddie."

"Yeah, Eddie Murphy. What did I say?"

"You said, 'Edie.'"

"Ah."

"But there're a lot of famous Murphys …"

My Murphy's head swerves each time she hears her name. I shake my head, lips turned downward, conveying: "I don't know any others."

" … Dale Murphy … "

I shake my head again.

"A baseball player," he snickers, "There's an Eddie Murphy who played baseball, too. 'Honest Eddie,' he was on the 1919 White Sox. The Black Sox."

"I see. I don't know a lot about baseball. There could be a thousand Murphys and I wouldn't know."

He laughs and says, "I was a huge fan as a kid. Less so now, but I still like to watch. Oh! Audie Murphy, the World War II soldier."

"Yeah, OK, I've heard of him. But Murphy's just Murphy. She's one of one."

He smiles, "I bet," and is patting her neck, looking back and forth between Murphy and me. "Yeah." Extending his hand for an air shake, "I'm Leo."

Because I am holding the leash, I respond with an upside-down left. "Gilmore."

He snickers again, "Murphy and Gilmore, two last names."

Gilmore is my last name as a matter of fact but I've liked it more than my first since childhood. Most of my family calls me Gilmore and those who don't call me "Gil." What my first name is, why I dislike it, the befuddled faces when I'm introduced as "Gil Gilmore" are some of my favorite stories, but telling a stranger everything about myself feels ridiculous. I let him think he is right, I smile and reply, "Ah, hadn't considered that," and tug a bit on Murphy's leash.

"Do you live in the neighborhood?" he asks.

"Yeah, I'm not too far from here, five-, ten-minute walk. You?"

"Yeah, same."

"Cool, cool …"

"Big cities are so weird," he says, "You can live in the same neighborhood as someone, hell on the same street, and never see them. Like living on different planets."

"Definitely. The same building, too. I'm surprised when I see the same face more than once."

"Oh, seeing the same person more than once is fate. That's the universe speaking."

I chuckle, "Maybe. Better than it being random."

Leo and I speak a few minutes longer. He is also a transplant, except Arizona in his case. I'd never met an Arizonian—well, not to my knowledge had I met a person from there—but, somehow, Leo is not what I unknowingly expect. When I think of the state, when I think of the entire region, I picture sweaty, slow-moving old people in baggy shorts, I picture toned, happy college students in flip-flops, I picture a fictional, cartoonish place where the sun doesn't set. I also remember one of the silliest quotes of all-time, "I am as American as April in Arizona," which I repeat to Murphy on our way home.

My first interaction with her had been similar to Leo's. This was a year earlier: after weeks of researching adoption, breeds, housetraining, and occasionally passing the shelter before finally going in. I was preparing for dog ownership, but also, I wanted to be certain how it would turn out. So I imagined myself with different breeds, which meant looking through the shelter's windows, sometimes lingering with smiles and waves, at other times barely making eye contact. When I ultimately stepped inside, however, the solidity of my daydreams disappeared. But, I guess, this should have been unsurprising because nothing prepares you for reality. The noise, for instance, the shelter was very noisy. I hadn't been inside one and could not tell if the dogs were begging to come home with me or wanting to attack someone for their confinement. A couple of them appeared to have lost their doggie minds and were barking and running in circles. I kept walking though and searching—while telling myself it was a mistake. A few minutes of disappointment had overwhelmed weeks of good feelings. Now the goal was forcing myself to perfunctorily see every dog before going home. This felt more mature than leaving partway: the dogs and humans would judge me less harshly if I walked the entire facility—although doing so was a put-on. Murphy's face was pressed against her cage. She looked at me, barked once, a low grumble then she barked again. This, I know, is how she voices impatience: she wanted me to adopt her. Murphy was taken from her cage and jumped on me; I started petting her, as happily as Leo would eventually. We took a walk that afternoon, which I remember because it's indistinguishable from those that followed. How we interacted with each other, our pace—not a hundredth of a second was different from the walks we have taken since.

Our next trips to the park we approached from the north, entering on Foster and ambling southward. I did not anticipate running into Leo but considered the possibility. When something interrupts your routine, part of you expects the same type of interruption to happen again. We make sense of the world through habit and few things are as habitual as walking your dog. But our walk in the park this afternoon is interrupted by a man peddling toward us. He is gangly, his bike is too small, his knees jut outwards, and with each revolution of the pedals, his discomfort causes him to swerve a little left, a little right. He starts waving, barely holding his line, which is when I notice the man is Leo. We step into the grass and he plods there, too, bouncing over the uneven field. Leo's bicycle is a cruiser, the light blue of Argentina's flag, which he lowers to the ground by the handlebar as though it were a ballet partner. His mask, still tucked beneath his nose, flaps in and out with each breath. I extends Murphy's leash so she can go to him. As he had before, Leo pets her as if they are old friends except he's sitting with crossed legs and notices my presence: "How's it going?"

I pause, reply, "Me or Murphy?"

"Ha! You. I know she's doing fine. Aren't you?"

"Good—all things considered. What about you?"

"Oh, same," he responds, "A dog would make it a little more fun, though, wouldn't it?"

His "wouldn't it?" is directed to Murphy but I answer: "You should get one, a dog. I think a lot of people are doing it now."

"I can imagine, but I don't have the space for a dog right now. You're pretty expensive, too, aren't you? Did I ask you how old she is? You said … "

"Two and a half but I've only had her about a year."

"Perfect timing, huh?"

If this is a serious question, it is, I think, directed to me. Leo uncrosses his legs and sits with them straight out. He is much taller than six feet, maybe six-foot-six or -seven, which remarkably, I had not noticed—even after he dismounted his bike. "Something like that," I answer, "I don't think anyone expected this to happen, but a year ago … Yeah. She won't know what to do when I have to go back to work."

Smiling, Leo answers, "Seriously," looks Murphy in the eyes and asks, "What're you gonna do, huh? What're you gonna do?" To me: "What did you do … for a living?"

"I work in communications—a communications specialist technically."

"You're a writer?"

"Not a 'writer-writer,'" I answer with emphasis. People often misunderstand my job this way, in part because I don't correct them forcefully enough. They hear my job title and think of their dreams and I want to dream a little with them. "Not a writer like you think. They're just articles for the company's intranet, short articles. I don't know, updates, keeping-morale-up type stuff."

He laughs and says, "OK," asks, "Where at?"

"The Partnership for Active Living, that professional associ-ation. It's physical therapists and dieticians …"

He nods, Murphy is sitting next to him as he rubs her head and back, "Yeah, yeah, I've heard of that, Partnership for Active Liv-ing. The building is nearby where I worked, yeah, I was in that area a lot."

"Where do you work?"

"I was at MG's."

"That diner, restaurant place? It sounds familiar. I think a lot of my coworkers liked going there."

"Yep, that's it, kind of a modern greasy spoon feel."

Involuntarily my knees bend a little as if part of me wants to sit in the grass, but I keep standing. "What do you do there?"

"I was a server."

"God, I could never do that job. I spent about twenty min-utes as a busboy in high school and couldn't handle it."

He is looking past Murphy, past his own feet and toward some spot in the grass. "It's hard but you get used to it, you know? Like anything else, you get better over time. You could pull off being a server if you needed to—decent money."

"I bet, with all the companies around there, especially for lunch and dinner."

"For sure, we stayed pretty busy." Leo turns, and with his

head, gestures at my free hand, which is tapping my leg unrhythmi-cally. "Drummer?"

I stop, look at my hand, then straighten my fingers to keep it still. "Oh, no, just jittery I guess. Didn't know I was doing that. You're a musician?"

"Not a 'musician-musician,'" he answers, "I was a band geek from, what, middle school through high school."

"What instrument?"

"Me, the mellophone. It's like a French horn."

I laugh, "I don't know either."

"Well, it's loud. I used to play in my apartment sometimes. My neighbors didn't appreciate that too much. They're pretty chill, though, so no one really complained. They'd just be like, 'Heard you rehearsing,' stuff like that."

Chuckling, I say, "I don't know, I don't think I'd like that either."

"Yeah, I know," Leo continues, "This was before the pan-demic. After all this happened, I played a few times, but it felt like a dickish thing to do. My girlfriend wasn't a fan either. She usually wasn't at home, but … then she was."

"Makes sense. Working from home changes a lot of things. Definitely did for me." I think of looking at my phone and lying about an upcoming meeting or video chat with my parents but in-stead ask, "What kind of music do you play?"

"My friends and I used to play kind of R&B-pop-jazz-y stuff."

Leo must see confusion on my face as I try to picture the sound of his music in my head because he asks, "Have you heard of The Dip?"

"Nah, not familiar with them."

He snickers and says, "Well, something like that but not to their level."

"Guess I'll have to look them up," I reply, "You played in clubs or just around?"

"We'd mostly just get together and jam."

I am fascinated by jamming, have my entire life, and want to know more. Who decides where you start? What are you thinking? When does a jam become a song? I never played or desired to play an instrument and Leo is the lone "musician-musician" I know (I clearly "know" him in a very loose sense, but he is a real musician whether he undersells himself or not). Leo takes out his phone and stares at it, however, and slowly, distractedly rubs Murphy from head to back. He stands and lifts his bike by a handlebar.

"Yeah, but not too often right now," he continues, eyeing his phone but answering me, "My girlfriend's trying to FaceTime, she's back in Arizona."

"Oh, no problem," I say, "See you around."

We absentmindedly reach for handshakes but pause midway and spend a few seconds false starting air shakes, pretend fist bumps, and fictional elbow taps. After swinging a leg over his bike, Leo leans down to pet Murphy's head. "You ever let her off the leash?" He's smirking, but I feel insecure. It's as if he said, "You're doing something wrong. She wants to run around"—and regardless, how would he know what Murphy wants?

I answer, "Sometimes, of course, when it's … " looking at the space between his right ear and shoulder, searching for the best words, " … when there's an enclosed space."

Leo kicks a peddle upward and presses his foot against it. "A friend of mine used to have a dog that he never leashed. Never. He used to say, 'A runaway dog is just looking for a better partner.' But who knows if that's true?" Testing his friend's theory might break my heart. Leo's phone is in his left hand. "See you around," he says and begins pedaling—bouncing and shifting his attention between FaceTime and the grass in front of him.

My bicycle is green, a shade of green that's a half-sibling to black, just four years old and rarely ridden nowadays. The summer I got it was a long, difficult one, too, though isolation those days was individual. Seclusion was called privacy when you spoke to someone in

2016—unless you were paying that person to listen. Obviously, that was also a summer of imagining a bleak future. For years, I had tried book clubs, language-practicing groups, mystifyingly a wine-tasting club (I prefer beer), a gardening group despite my superpower for killing plants. But teachers and my mother, who also spent the brightest months in darkness, had always noted my perseverance. I joined a bicycling group in a neighborhood where I didn't live that summer and bought my first bike since childhood. Weeks before our first meeting, I would position myself in a doorframe, balancing as long as I could before reaching for the walls, and acclimated to riding again pedaling through bumpy fields. I fell down occasionally but practiced in hidden-away areas, so I would not know if onlookers had seen me. The group's first ride was a Saturday morning, early and cool enough to make the eventual midday heat and humidity feel like another country. We met at the park. About a dozen of us came—not enough people to avoid being seen—but I survived by introducing myself, listening to them speak, and positioning toward the back when our ride started. I also persisted because I could leave anytime. That I could peel away from the group and be left with no less than what I had before kept me going. The worst, as I knew, was not unbearable. We pedaled and there was often between me and someone else an exchange of smiles, most times just an exchange of smiles, because they wanted to be nice but did not know what to make of me. Understandable—I felt similarly. Our ride was nearer to the beginning than I thought when Rosa appeared at my side. Her bicycle was brownish-orange and had bullhorn handlebars. I noticed she had one break. Rosa's messenger bag was grey with black straps, her helmet was black with two orange stripes down its center, and both were well-worn, battered, and scuffed-up in ways that gave her character: you saw them and assumed she had incredible stories to tell. A man towing an empty child trailer noticed her, smiled, and waved. Seconds later she said to me, "Not too late, I was able to catch up," her eyebrows jumped once excitedly. I heard slurping, hard candy rattling against teeth, and Rosa's lips were rolling and pursing when I glanced, her cheeks stretching one way then another. "Is this your first ride?" she asked.

"Yeah, my first one, but I've been wanting to do it for a while," I answered somewhat truthfully. "A while" is an ambivalent phrase, though I suspect the psychological time between idea and arrival stretched much longer for me than most others. "You, your first time?"

"Oh, no, no, I've done plenty of these. In different neighborhoods, too," she said, smacking her lips between sentences. Ends of black hair were sticking from beneath her helmet, Rosa's nose was small, round, and she was as thin as a healthy person could be, "They have them all over the city. I started with this group because it's where I live."

"That's cool," I responded.

How you remember someone is inseparable from how you met them. My oldest souvenir about Rosa is that she was more comfortable on her bicycle than I was on my feet. That was the first day I saw her pedal while looking backwards without veering sideways, pointing to a shop or frontage she did not know was there. Countlessly I also saw Rosa sit up, legs churning, and maneuver the messenger bag to her chest: she would take out one of her beloved butterscotch candies, pop it in her mouth, and stuff the wrapper away. She resembled a daredevil to me. I was impressed by her acrobatics. In that way, Rosa and I were unalike. I was most secure with eyes in front and fingers clutching the handlebars: I needed a red light to drink water. But in ways that mattered, she and I were kin. Meeting her rekindled my childhood belief, against all evidence and family denials, that I was adopted and a real family existed in the world for me. The details of our lives were different, but the essence was identical. She was from a nearby suburb, socialized more easily than me, but Rosa and I had in common moods of homelessness and a resigned distrust of the future. Yet, we also shared an inchoate, unspoken desire that our emotional futures not resemble our emotional pasts. Too predictably, we also enjoyed macabre humor.

Much later I realized how we'd stayed in each other's orbits that Saturday, during the ride and when the group gathered afterward for goodbyes. The following week, she and I talked in the park after the others dispersed, and the next week, when the group had tired, we ventured to another neighborhood. Although Rosa was a much better, more dedicated rider than me—when the weather allowed, she biked everywhere—the foundation of our friendship was riding bicycles. "You know, if you actually moved to my neighborhood," she said, "you wouldn't be an interloper in the group." We'd met almost a year before, my lease was nearly up. Our cycling group was alive but fading away.

"I'm sure no one cares," I responded.

"You don't know what we say behind your back."

It was the first time in life I had not a friend but a close friend, not a close friend but a close friend who lived nearby. I remember exhaustion after one of our adventures, sitting on the Cultural Center's floor and staring at its Tiffany Dome. Rosa had led me there circuitously—west-southwest then southeast—and as I sat, foolishly nervous my sweat would ruin the building, she was taking pictures on a self-guided tour. I wanted to go with her but was drained, gulping water and stretching my legs when I was sure they wouldn't be in other peoples' way. Rosa was smirking when she reappeared and I dreaded riding someplace else, but she stopped a step or so in front of me and rested her phone atop a curled index finger, held it stationary with her thumb and palm. Pointing the phone at my face, tilting her head and shutting an eye, she said, "The coup de grâce," and made a childish-sounding gun noise that resembled a rocket launch more than a firearm. I flung my arms and body as though I had been electrocuted, held my breath and lay motionless on the floor.

She said, "Meet me at Mariano's. I need to get … " I don't remember what she needed but knew I would not see her bike when I arrived. With these kinds of trips, brief and for things she could fit in her bag, Rosa took it inside—carrying it up stairways, standing alongside her bicycle on escalators, maneuvering it through aisles and into elevators. "Thank god for self-checkout," she once told me, "Squeezing through checkout used to be a pain in the ass." She'd convinced me that our first ride of 2019 would be long and chilly: to the botanic garden in the liminal days of autumn and spring. Concerning my stamina and tolerance for riding in the still-unkind air, I was unprepared, but the rest of me was ready. I arrived and waited. Rosa, unusually, did not respond to my text. As I experienced that day, waiting and searching for her took hours, though realistically, it must not have been more than five or ten minutes. I locked my bike to search inside, going to where I would most likely find her: near the bananas and apples, the candy aisle, but quickly decided the better idea was waiting near self-checkout. That was short-lived, too. I had buried myself behind abandoned grocery carts when I remembered the front doors: she would have to pass me there. But rather than walking to the exit, I lurched toward it with a suspicious-looking half-jog—breathing heavily, struggling to zip my jacket—hurrying down the escalator as if its tide would reverse and sweep me back into the store. Someone might easily, understandably have suspected unpaid-for trifles were shoved in my pants. Plowing through the revolving door, I tripped, then fumbled my bike lock open and headed to her apartment, retracing the path I knew she would have taken: Damen was straight, better paved, I could picture her, hands free and unwinding her legs, smiling into the air. Instead I saw an ambulance, onlookers, police near the intersection with Ainslie. I immediately reassured myself. This is a distraction, I thought, I'm looking for my best friend who's oversleeping or so ill she can't get out of bed. In my replay of what happened, I tell myself to keep going as I also told myself that morning, but my retelling cannot escape reality. I want to continue but slow until I stop. Most bystanders were at the intersection's southwest corner. With my bike, I ran between the front and rear bumpers of two cars at a stop sign. A vehicle heading south stopped in the middle of the street when I flashed in front of it. I pushed myself close to a couple and looked over their heads:

"What happened?" Neither responded but the woman was holding a child's hand. She felt him tug away, looked at him: "No, put that down. Where'd you get that? Don't eat things you find outside." My head and eyes moved everywhere, but it was make-believe looking. I wanted the scene to be another person's problem, so I could not find what I feared. The man turned to me and said, "I think that car hit somebody on a bike." He pointed to a mauve-colored hatchback with a scraped and dented hood, a cracked windshield. It resembled a battered and broken-toothed boxer smiling after a victorious fight. When my head and eyes slowed and honestly focused on everything around me, I saw, as close as she would be on our rides when she sped up and looked over her shoulder to make sure I had not been left behind, Rosa's mangled bike.

Three weeks pass without seeing Leo. Murphy and I again enter from the park's north when someone starts playing a horn. Although I believe it's coming from the park, I'm unsure and I also have no way of discerning a mellophone from a sax or trumpet. Possibly for the first time my pace hurries Murphy, my ears overruling her nose. We make it to the park's southeast corner and walk westward through the grass. The music is coming from the park: still too far away to make out who, the person is sitting and playing a few seconds at a time as if they're trying to re-figure out the instrument. I walk faster and once or twice stop Murphy from lingering on a nondescript patch of grass. But that person is not Leo. When I get close enough to say his name, a teenager looks up. I think he's playing a kind of tuba.

In novels there's a trope wherein people return years, decades after they left. Erstwhile friends and exes come back, open-hearted and contrite, wanting to repair and reconnect. Or if they've died, a memento from your time together boomerangs into your possession. I never believed this, however, and have no reason to believe it now. People don't return. They are here today and gone before sunset. Goodbyes are final. People move and move on. I will not run into Leo again or read his name in an obit and start a search through his life to understand why we met there and then. He is as past as my best friend Rosa. But having met Leo, even for a short time, I can now think about our encounters, which is more important than most people understand: how long we survive this life ultimately depends on the force of our memories.

Fragments of a Lost Patient

I would set my clients up with each other?

No, I'm not talking about *you* setting up people *you* work with directly. I'm talking about something bigger. I'm talking about a dating service run by therapists. You and a bunch of other therapists would set your patients up with each other. Therapists would use what they know to send people on dates. That's the most important part. That's how the business works: you know everything about us, why not match people by emotional well-being? Their neuroses? I can envision some of your patients being set up, but that's not the point.

OK. Before our conversation made this turn, he'd withdrawn from the room. The more he spoke—or, frankly, tried to speak—the more I lost contact with him. Nothing was keeping him present or engaged, and each fragment and half-sentence he uttered with shrugs and exhales that asked for attention but concealed his emotions. After a few minutes of rubbing his hands together and looking everywhere but my face, Anthony started talking about his idea. He became excited, his eyes widened and his hands waved like an overheated politician.

It's a good idea, right? Better than apps we have now. It makes a lot more sense in terms of meeting someone and staying with that person. You have to know what really attracts you to other people and drives you away from them, too. Everybody is … Wanna know what I call it?

Finish that thought.

Which thought—about the dating service?

No, you said, Everybody is, and stopped.

I don't remember what I was about to say. Do you want to know the name?

Sure, what is it?

Head and Heart.

Uh-huh.

In the logo, the *e* in, Head, is shaped like a little brain. Or, no, like a little cranium—in profile, you see what I mean? The forehead pointing to the left. Anthony turned his head to his left and to his right. He continued, And in, Heart, the *a* is a little heart.

Uh-huh, I see. Let's pause here.

When you have more to say, it ends, he added, When you have nothing to say, it never stops. I remember smiling and Anthony smiling. He said, Head and Heart could be your way out of here. You could retire a millionaire.

You want me to stop working?

Everyone wants to stop working.

I replied, Alright: that's a perfect transition, because I want to remind you that I'll be out the next couple of weeks.

I learned from the best. Yeah, I remembered. See you in three weeks.

We stood and Anthony rotated his watch to the topside of his wrist. He wore a long-sleeved, red button-up shirt with light green stripes and blue, slim-fitting dress pants. His over-the-shoulder bag and fleece jacket were hanging from the same hook on the coat rack beside him. At the end of each session, no matter the weather or season, Anthony took whatever he'd brought with him and removed at the beginning of our session—winter coat, backpack, scarf—into his hands as if he could not or was not allowed to put them on inside the consulting room. Indeed, I answered, But if you need anything, I'll be available.

Anthony smiled a bit more and said, See you in three weeks.

See you then.

Before the door shut I heard Anthony, steps away, dropping his bag to the floor and rustling into his jacket.

I wanted to doze the entire flight to Lisbon, but instead spent eight hours suspended just above the baptismal waters of sleep. It was early afternoon in America and my eyes were shut. I couldn't sleep, however, because the sudden mantra, It'll be tomorrow when we land, It'll be tomorrow when we land, colonized my reclining head. But despite my annoyance at being awake, I appreciated, as I never had, how time zones alter perceptions. Crossing the Atlantic was escaping what it meant for me to be alive in the United States. Emotionally, the Lisbon of my mind was farther away than any place I'd visited, with life happening under a different regime of past and present. I have known many people with radiant, practically garish, imaginations, but the future, to me, was cataloged rather than pictured. My Lisbon daydreams, though, were like watching the future play in advance. I would sleep a few hours in the clothes I was wearing, long enough to tell myself I rested. Then, without showering, grab my side bag, put on clean socks and my seven-year-old running sneakers, the only shoes I brought and the most comfortable, trustworthy pair I own. The city feels crowded already, but getting lost doesn't worry me. I'm OK. The sun causes my eyes to squint and I refuse to go back for my shades. I tell myself, You're OK, and cross the street to Luís de Camões Square.

His monument, a 21,000-pound cast-bronze statue, is first on the agenda that maps out my future. People are talking on nearby benches while others cross the plaza. A young man is sitting on the statue's base and tracing his phone's screen with a middle finger as he reads. I take a picture, and unlike myself, also grab a cloudburst of images as I approach. de Camões is wearing a crown of laurels, wielding a sword, and clutching *The Lusiads* at his chest. At the poet's feet are eight others from Portugal's history, most of whom were idealized by the sculptor because portraits could not be found. The young man puts his phone away and leaves. I step where he was sitting and touch the plinth of the person we're told is Fernão Lopes. King Duarte, the philosopher-king, appointed him to chronicle Portugal's monarchy in 1434. Of Lopes, *Encyclopedia Britannica* says he, Occupies a special place in medieval historiography because he held that the surest way of arriving at historical truth was through the evidence of historical documents. He and I are closer than the centuries separating our lives. From that morning, when I took an early train to walk beaches in Cascais, until the end of my vacation, I saw almost every place I wanted but surprised myself by happily not seeing every place I planned. Intentions changed after Rua Augusta Arch, which in my pre-Lisbon past would have been hardly possible. If I carried regrets home, I knew they wouldn't be places unseen but not going there sooner, not on days one or two in Lisbon but my third. I went back countlessly. How I experienced myself in that city was unlike any other spot on Earth. The first visit I arrived doubly relieved after losing and finding my way to the National Museum of Contemporary Art, where I showed up before it opened, then losing and finding my way to the Arch. I walked back and forth across its entrance, fixated, without dropping my head. Directly above me, in relief, was Portugal's coat of arms. On the Arch's southwest were statues of Viriathus, leader of the Lusitanian resistance to Roman invasion during the second century BCE, Vasco de Gama, the first European to reach India by ocean, and lounging godlike, an allegory of the Tagus River. A personification of the Douro River, the Marquis of Pombal, chief minister to King Joseph I and de facto ruler of Portugal from 1750-1777, and Nuno Álvares Pereira, canonized military leader in their centuries-old wars for independence, were memorialized in statues on the Arch's southeast. Atop the Arch were three more figures. Standing tallest, on a throne of three steps, was Glory, twenty-three feet high and holding crowns above the heads of Valor to her right and Genius to her left. Beneath them an inscription said, To the virtues of the greatest, so that it serves all of teaching. I finally crossed the monument's threshold and saw its clock, embraced by majestic, filigreed stone relief, opposite the coat of arms. Through the archway, in Commerce Square, I noticed the Equestrian Statue of King Joseph I and walked toward it. His monument reaches forty-five feet. The monarch, who we're told, Was content to leave decisions to his ministers, devoting himself to his pleasures, had been adorned with a cape and plumed helmet while horseback and gazing southward at the Tagus River. Snakes were placed at his feet as were images of conquest on the pedestal beneath him, Fame and Triumph driving an elephant and horse over human depictions. Even at the time, it was bizarre to me that here I genuinely, unmistakably first heard languages other than Portuguese. English. German. Russian. What I thought was Korean. Many people were speaking what sounded like Spanish or Italian. I most often spent my visits strolling through Commerce Square, where King Carlos I was assassinated, or ambling and sitting in the Pier of Columns to its south. I imagined swimming into the Tagus River and giddily reaching the other shore. I also remembered, consistently so, the earthquake of 1755. Tens of thousands died in collapsed buildings, fires, the tsunami that came ashore. All the architectural beauty around me was built after great destruction. My vacation ended. I had an evening flight home. When the plane reached some indeterminate spot over the Atlantic, I repeatedly thought, It'll be yesterday when we land, It'll be yesterday when we land.

A client once told me, Bad news finds you. I guessed her to be about my mother's age when we met, but she was forty-five, young enough to be my big sister. Life had been long, difficult, so when I usually thought of her, I wondered how she was doing and hoped, if nothing else, circumstances hadn't worsened since our treatment ended. But her statement occurred to me because my return from Lisbon seemed to validate its truth. From plane's touchdown that evening through my waking up the next morning, I was unaware of what happened to Anthony. Perhaps, I was refusing to depart Lisbon and restart life in the Midwest. It's a convincing theory, because once I saw the news, I couldn't avoid hearing and reading that high waves had swept thirty-nine-year-old teacher Anthony Glass into Lake Michigan. On the morning I saw the report, Anthony had been missing two days. I was making coffee. The television played in the background. His name was muffled initially—or I heard it as such, so I went to the TV and rewound it. In reverse, I saw a reporter along the lakefront trail with an anemic Chicago sky, a man-on-the-street interviewee, the reporter once more, a headshot of Anthony appear next to an anchor and fade into a Walter E. Smithe commercial. I let the newscast play in the direction of time. National Weather Service Chicago had issued a high-wave warning the day he disappeared. It forecasted waves twelve to eighteen feet and gusts of wind forty to forty-five miles an hour. A person who lived nearby said it looked dangerous. Anthony's life was more important to me than it was to the city. Regardless, the news segments I watched and articles I read felt cold-heartedly brief, and practically each said he was, Feared missing, as though he might reappear in another county. Anthony, as everyone who cared about him knew, was dead.

Before he walked through my door, Anthony was flexing his right wrist and hand and wiggling those fingers. It was noticeable then distracting. I don't recall how long it took for me to realize my attention had been uneven for much of the session. The continual supinating and pronating of his wrist and occasional grimace also angered me. Say it! I wanted to order him, Say whatever it is you want. Directly. Please. But no more sign language. I asked, What happened to your hand?

I don't know. I'm almost forty, he responded. Anthony's fingers uncoiled repeatedly, as though he was flicking snot at me, Shit just hurts sometimes.

There's always a reason, I answered. My inflection was airy, I think of it, in retrospect, as having been tender, affectionate.

You believe that more than I do. You wake up and it's your back or your hips and there's no reason, except you're older. This didn't happen in my twenties. Or, if it did, I wouldn't have noticed.

He stopped, wanting me to respond, but instead, I listened. Anthony rolled his eyes and looked away from me, Anyway, you get paid to believe if A then B, but like was I saying before you asked about my hand …

CNN published a video report the Wednesday Anthony was lost. I found it while searching for information about conditions that afternoon and evening. It's a minute and twenty seconds of pensive music, muted colors, and waves collapsing onto people along the lakefront. It starts with an older man jogging then pausing and moving close to a concrete revetment as water strikes him. This precedes the first unnarrated caption, A strong storm caused heavy winds and towering waves in Chicago. Surfers, I hardly remembered surfing existed in the Midwest, but the video shows them riding muddy-colored waves, and another caption, People were advised to stay away from Lake Michigan due to deadly swimming conditions. At thirty-four seconds, two people are running. The young man is shirtless, wearing black shorts, pink sneakers, and is steps in front of his companion, a young woman in white sneakers, black tank top, and shorts matching the pink of his shoes. Her strides are short, choppy, the heels of her feet hit the ground first. The guy runs on his toes and gallops with high knees. He's looking to his right, but watching the first time, I couldn't tell if he is cautiously eyeing the lake or trying to keep her in his peripheral vision. The ground she's trusting abruptly becomes water, she falls, the wave ricochets and rises off the retaining wall and engulfs her. He notices, stops, and when she reemerges, the water is carrying her to him but she's facing the opposite direction. Next, at a third section of lakefront, I see two men walking with bicycles, the second of whom is drenched by a wave as he records the danger. I'm upset because neither is Anthony and because the helpless cyclist survives. Nevertheless, despite my years in the city, I can only figure out their location. The Hancock Center briefly appears in the background and I know they are just south of where Anthony was last seen. I momentarily wonder if they might have crossed paths. It's a familiar area, close to a popular beach, a stretch of trail where the pavement slants toward Lake Michigan. On perfect, sunny days it can be unsettling to walk or bike so close to a massive body of water atop uneven ground. Absolutely, I tell myself, his death was accidental.

Everything I read and watched said Anthony's appearance and demeanor that day were typical. Nobody worried about his condition, and in fact, a colleague recounting their conversation before he left said of him, He seemed fine. Anthony used public transportation but walked to a station much farther away to avoid seeing students from his school. He doggedly wanted the space between work and home to be free of obligations to either. An article I found includes stills captured from a video feed of Anthony entering one station and exiting another. Foul play, in reporter- and cop-speak, was not suspected. Besides those images, Anthony had successfully, by his definition, faded unnoticed into a crowd of anonymous commuters. Even so, a local television station interviewed a woman who claimed to have seen him. She and her dog had been walking at the top of a three-step revetment. The dog noticed Anthony first and began tugging toward him with its ears and tail erect. He's definitely the guy I've seen on TV, the woman said, There was something going on with him. The man she observed was stoutly built, had little hair except for his beard, had rolled up his sleeves, and carried a bag in his hand, all of which was unexceptional. But he walked closely, slowly to the water that sometimes came ashore and wetted his feet and legs. She added, We were going south, the same direction, but it looked so bad I hurried out. It was eerie. These big waves kept coming in and missing him. I don't think he was paying a lot of attention. Now I wish I said something. Maybe, you know, he needed that?

You're right: I do feel that way when I sense you're withholding, when a part of you is disengaged.

You withhold, too, but you withhold everything from me.

I don't mean what I said as a punishment or criticism—

Sure, he interrupted.

What would you like to know?

This entire, he paused, Whatever you call it between us, is phony. Anthony's hands were opened, raised, extended in front of his chest, and moving in circles as if he were slowly gathering bills to himself in a money machine. He continued, I come in and talk and talk and you take. That's what bothers me: you take but you don't give back. I don't know one iota about you. Well, I know you're a therapist and some unthreatening stuff, but this isn't an authentic relationship.

I asked, What would an authentic relationship be like?

Putting his hands down, Reciprocation, he answered.

What else?

I don't know. It's impossible.

It's not possible to have an authentic relationship?

Yes.

Why isn't that possible?

Because it's inappropriate. We can't do anything but sit here and listen to me talk. You can't even say how you really feel about me.

Is it your desire to have an inappropriate relationship?

This is pointless.

I rewatched and reread the same news stories and did little else that day. His death, I refused to think of him as missing, was deeply saddening. In more than a decade of practice, once had a client died: a woman in her early seventies who'd come to me years into cancer treatment. She and I spent twenty-three months together, knowing, eventually, illness wouldn't allow her to continue. When it happened, I was heartsick. Her first missed session meant we'd seen each other the last time. But grief and mourning had been part of our work from the beginning: implicitly and explicitly she and I prepared for her dying. Anthony's death, on the other hand, was unexpected, baffling, cruel. I told him, If you need anything, I'll be available, and he responded, See you in three weeks. I know he believed me. I know

I believed him. Yet, Anthony died two days before I returned and days before our next appointment. I was angry, too. His leaving this life caused him to dominate mine. Instead of re-finding my routine of living, I was thinking of him, what transpired during my absence, if I'd missed a clue he provided, ultimately asking myself, Was my vacation a mistake? And that guilt-ridden question pissed me off. I needed time away and his death threatened stealing that sustenance from me. Taking off was not a crime, and as a matter of fact, he could have called, texted whenever he needed. My holiday was never at the expense of his well-being. I looked forward to our sessions. Why do something reckless? Anthony, use your words.

I opened the counseling room's door and saw Anthony seated facing me. He usually picked a chair outside my immediate sight: I customarily had to step into the waiting area to see him. Anthony's head was down, a phone was in his hand, an inverted peace sign jumped Double Dutch atop his leg. Music often came up during our sessions, especially what songs he loved and how they made him feel, though he rarely did more than move close to the emotions they provoked without grazing their skin. But I'd never seen him listening to it, enjoying himself. He looked up and approached with out-of-character energy.

Skipping our normal pleasantries, I haven't heard this in years, Anthony started, You know the song Wah-Wah? His question had been asked with such quickness that I wasn't able to cross my legs. My right knee paused mid-flight then completed its motion as I tried to connect title and tune. Like me, he was still organizing himself, moving about to put his earbuds and phone away. I replied uncertainly, Wah-Wah? I don't think so.

Anthony shimmied his watch to the inside of his wrist—the lone occasion I witnessed him turn its face downward. Before that evening and thereafter, I observed the move's reversal when our sessions ended, but excitement had caused him to forget his normal preparation. Likewise, Anthony's exuberance evoked the same in me. I leaned toward him emotionally. We entered a third space wearing the same smile. George Harrison, he replied.

I answered, No, I don't think I've heard it.

Really? he said, Might be a little obscure but I figured you would know. Anthony reached for the pocket where he'd stashed his phone and paused: I started to play it. Maybe I shouldn't. Anyway, I remember listening to him a lot as a teenager, especially that song. I don't know how long it's been since … He's not what I listen to nowadays, as you know, but that was big for me as a younger person. He snickered, I took pride in that, too. Nobody my age, no negroes my age especially, were listening to George Harrison in the late-90s—John or Paul either, I'm sure.

I don't believe you've mentioned this song before.

Probably not. I can't remember when I last thought about it.

Why'd you think of it today?

Yeah, I don't know. I'm trying to recall.

He looked up, ostensibly in thought, toward a familiar corner of the wall to my upper left and stared. Anthony stroked his face, pulling its skin downward from eyes to chin. His enthusiasm was waning as was mine. With each unhurried, wordless repetition of that gesture, his visage appeared more ghoulish. He wanted to escape from what had been stirred up, and if he did, that evening, like countless more, would be spent trying to recapture what we almost possessed. I interjected, Why was the song important when you were a teenager?

My dad hated it, he answered. Anthony's hand fell onto his lap. His eyes swooped from the ceiling and past me as if he'd lost where I was in the room before making eye contact. I liked the song, really liked, before I discovered how much he detested it, but his hostility pushed me, too. I didn't know the song's meaning, and maybe I don't now, but I felt it was about being unhappy and him making me unhappy, but also making fun of him for being unhappy, and he knew that. I'd start playing it or singing it when he was already a little irritated. But you'd never know with him. He was

Cliff Huxtable for a week then, who? Lex Luthor or somebody for another week. My bed, for instance, would be unmade for days. I was a teenager. Whatever. It's inexplicable. Regardless, something would be a certain way for days, and on day whatever, he would go insane. Screaming. Yelling. Marching. Spit flying. Literal spit flying. I'm not saying that to—as a metaphor. Literal spit flying. Vietnam, drill sergeant, boot camp shit. And he'd have his fists clenched, so you had in your mind, This dude might—Who knows what might happen? It was just me and my mom at this point. My brother had moved out years before—years before these memories. I'm sure he experienced the same stuff and I'm not remembering when I was younger right now. You could tell by how the door sounded when he came home, how his footsteps sounded. You would know: he's in a bad mood. I used to ask myself a lot, Did he shoot someone today? I'd check the news to see if a cop had shot somebody. He was in Vietnam, too— You know this—but that … Anthony stopped. It differed from his earlier breaking off, however. He was finding the words and means to continue. I accompanied the silence. Eighteen or nineteen, he restarted, Eighteen-nineteen when he went to Vietnam. Eighteen. His brother, Uncle Bobby, went, too. I never met him. He was younger than my dad by a year. He, Uncle Bobby I'm talking about, followed my dad. They're all secondhand stories to me, but apparently he really looked up to my dad, but also wanted to best him. Siblings. We know about … siblings. My dad was drafted into the Army, so Uncle Bobby joined the Marines. Anthony stopped again and pulled his face down again. He continued, I compare his mood swings to ripping a shirt open—I don't know if you've ever tried this—like Superman. Maybe it's just something boys do, but the hardest part is getting it going. The first rip. When you do, it gets easier until the last threads are left. That's where the shirt regains some give and you really have to work and tug to yank it apart. I don't know what he saw over there, what he did, but I feel that's what happened to him. He's been living for decades with a few stubborn threads connected. Uncle Bobby's came loose, I bet … My mom is just hanging on, too. She's probably no healthier. I'm talking about emotionally and psychologically. She's less trigger-able, if that's a word, but … they've been together for decades. And you can't fake time. I wonder how they got along in private, though. Or before my brother was born. Or now even with both us out of the house. I remember her being there while this maniac was, what, being a maniac, and she would just be quiet. I figured she was afraid of what might happen, and I still think she was, but maybe she knew to wait him out. Couples know each other better than their kids know them. Maybe that was how they loved. Anthony turned away, grinning with one cheek as though he'd recalled the face of a grade school playmate. Then he said, Hearing that song would have set me off, too.

Miracle. This tiny, irrational word erupted in my head when I saw Anthony's body had been discovered and I don't know why. Letters in that order, producing that sound are a temple of illogic. Much of what happens in life is difficult to understand but none of it is miraculous. Whenever I hear these words, I think card tricks and saints materializing in foods, not a body washing ashore at a beach close to where the person was last spotted. Certainly none of what transpired was wondrous or extraordinary. In reality, life can often make too much sense. Our universe is faithful to its rules and that's what makes it hard to live, that is its absurdity. Anthony had been missing a week. The day his corpse was found I'd heard helicopters around noon from my Loop office but dismissed them as big-city background noises. Though as life dictates, the discovery found me: it led all the local evening news broadcasts. Repeating the same phrase, passersby said they saw an object that, Looked like a body, and reporters again reiterated, Foul play, was not suspected. One of them had even called Anthony's death, A tragic accident, before sending *it*—his life and death and their momentary concern—to the studio where Anthony Glass would be forgotten. Amnesia was not an option for me. Sometime during the first months after he started therapy, Anthony had said, It's strange. Our, whatever you call it, relationship, it's strange because it resembles a lot of other kinds of relationships but isn't any of them. In different ways, he repeated that sentiment for years. I have loved all my clients, though naturally, some more than others. But his presence, because he was not quite a memory yet, had broken through whatever personal-professional boundary I thought existed, and I felt his words realized inside me. It was a rare type of grief and regret, as if someone of undefinable closeness had died.

It did not shock the practitioner in me that my own therapist seemed useless. He is a kind, patient man who I have thanked more than appropriate but less than he deserves. Nevertheless, I was, for a time, no longer convinced of his ability or our connection and re-member sitting across from him and thinking, He can't help, which was contrary to everything I'd learned, ostensibly believed, and told others. But I continued going, and although each session my eyes led to the door, I didn't leave. History kept me in the room. Somehow, though, when I began assembling fragments of the past, I couldn't tell if this exact instant of anti-therapy gloom was after Anthony's death or earlier—like an email you know you received but cannot find. Yet, when it's finally tracked down, some events are given order. I can separate this period from others because of the pearly-grey row in my inbox with Janie G. between a yellow star and an unas-suming subject line, Hello, talking some time. Anthony's mother, whom I'd never communicated with, had contacted me to ask if she and I and Anthony's father could speak. I told my therapist about her email. Before responding, his head tilted backward as though he were driving into a miniature sunset, he then asked, How do you feel about that? I said: they're going to blame me for his death. I said: they want to tell me I failed their son. I said: no, they want to tell me I ruined their son. I said: they're going to say Anthony was fine until he started therapy. I said: they're going to say I could've done more. I said: maybe none of that is true. I said: they're going to ask if I noticed any difference. I said: they want to know what he last said to me. I said: they're angry. I said: they're sad. I said: they need someone to blame other than themselves. I said: they want to know if I believe he intended to die. I said: I can't predict the future. I said: they're grieving. I said: part of me wants to speak with them, too. I said: they should feel guilty. I said: they hate me. I said: I don't think he intended to die. I said: they want to know if he was depressed. I said: it might be good for me, too. I said: I don't know what he was thinking. I said: they're right, I'm not good at my job. I said: we process loss differently. I said: Portugal had been nice. I said: his parents are dubious figures. I said: had I never come back … I said: had I never come back … I said: had I never come back … I said: had I never come back … I cried. I cried. I kept crying.

Margaret, two and two is four, but every number isn't a two.

What are you trying to communicate?

He hesitated, I don't know yet.

Before meeting Anthony's parents, I used *them* and *they*, I thought of Janie and Hank as a unit. I presumed, although exchanging emails with Janie, that she spoke for the couple and the couple acted collectively. Along with them, we settled on a Thursday afternoon. They said getting together online would be easier. But a strong woman and a very frail man emerged on my computer screen. The Hank of today was in his seventies and looked as though he'd left Vietnam that morning. He was gaunt and his eyes strayed as if they were following his mind leave the room. Given what I knew of Hank, I anticipated being furious, I prepared myself not to be intimidated by him, but I didn't encounter that man. Time had taken from Hank much of the force he possessed, and whatever it left was diminished greatly. It was demanding, imaginatively speaking, to take the pieces in front of me and reconstruct the bully I knew he'd been. Whereas I felt pressing a finger into Hank would burst through his skin as though it were rotten tomato, Janie was a solid person, self-assured, and in control of herself and her husband. Hank, in his baggy short-sleeved shirt and askew baseball cap, owed that he was still alive to

Janie, who was bundled in a scarf and sweater. She wore a light red lipstick and periodically sipped a glass of water.

We'd like to thank you for speaking with us, she said, We know you'd been working with Anthony, so we thought you'd have some insight about what happened.

I hope I can be helpful, I answered, I will do what I can, but I'm afraid there might not be much I can offer.

She replied, I understand. Anything you have is valuable.

Janie's voice was soft, even-keeled, but without weakness. Mine seemed frail, as though parts of my vocal cords were dying out. Before we go further, could I ask you all a question?

Sure, anything.

What was Anthony's childhood like? How was he as a kid?

He was a very sweet child, Janie answered. When someone says, This person didn't have an enemy in the world, that was Anthony. People liked him. He was a normal kid. I would say, yes, a normal kid. When Anthony was a teenager, he was a little moody, as they all can be. Minor things would aggravate him, Janie said, snapping her fingers. Hank had been nodding as Janie spoke and, when she finished, he added, Anthony definitely had friends. A very normal young man. His brother was the same way. Janie looked at him as if only to acknowledge he'd spoken before turning to me. Yes, his brother was that way, too, she said, The Glass men are the same. She wistfully looked at Hank but he'd left the room again.

Were he and his brother close?

Well, Janie said, yes. But Michael is ten years older, so it was tough for them to be in the same place at the same time. When Michael was a teenager, Anthony was a little boy, and he'd moved away by the time Anthony was a teenager. They were close, though. I think, more recently, they were really starting to build an even closer relationship. I believe the years between them were starting to feel shorter.

I responded, That makes sense. They were both adults. A

twenty-year old and a ten-year old are farther apart than a forty-year old and a fifty-year old.

Exactly.

I'm sorry but you said when Anthony was a teenager he could be moody, how so? Did he do anything that worried you?

Janie opened her mouth, but it took a heartbeat for words to follow. No, he never worried us at all, she answered, Whatever silly things he did were no different from other people his age. I say that, but obviously, we don't know what Anthony told you. She conveniently drew a breath and drank water as if cueing me to play my section of song. But I didn't respond, and she continued, He would try to stay out later than we allowed, for example. He thought we were too strict. Stuff you expect from young people. And we'd seen all of it with Michael, so there weren't many surprises with Anthony. Did he mention issues with the way we raised him?

I, I can't divulge, naturally, what Anthony and I discussed, but he was a complicated person. Like all of us, he brought experiences from childhood into adulthood. Those are formative times.

Janie responded, Yes, that's reasonable, but we're not asking for personal details. You must sympathize with our position. Our baby is dead and we don't know why and we just want to be able to make sense out of what happened.

I thought, She believes Anthony killed himself. Without evidence, I had assumed she was convinced as I was convinced: that Anthony behaved dangerously but did not want to die. I do sympathize with your position, I responded, sensing in real-time I was pleading for her belief, But I can't reveal what someone has told me.

Hank, who kept looking down and away from their computer screen, interjected, You won't catch me crying.

Patting his arm, Janie said, Hank, please.

I continued, It's hard to comprehend, for me as well.

Janie smirked, repeated, For me as well.

The anxiety was if thousands of microscopic people were

haphazardly fleeing a bomb blast inside my torso and I could feel their tiny steps and hear all their teeny screams. I said, I'm sorry, I didn't mean to appropriate or … minimize your loss.

Janie replied, I know you didn't. We just want to be able to comprehend why this happened. That's all.

Plaintively, I said, Me, too, and feared I had trivialized their grief.

But, looking at me, Janie said, Anthony seeing you meant a lot to him. He told us how much good it was doing. You must be hurt by this, too.

I wanted to speak but every word stopped at the top of my throat.

We don't blame you, Janie continued, Believe me: we don't. I'm angry at the world and a part of me is mad at Anthony, but it's not your fault. She leaned forward and a hand rose toward her computer, distinctive signs our meeting had ended.

I'm sorry I couldn't be more helpful.

Don't be, you've done a lot. Thank you again for speaking with us.

No, thank you.

She smiled, Bye-bye.

You haven't talked a lot about your relationship. My impression is it's been important.

How so? Like, are we close?

What comes to mind?

Of course. Well, Michael, as you know, is ten years older than me, so I don't remember much from my childhood. It's strange because, and maybe this is true and maybe it isn't, but usually when two siblings are that far apart in age, they have other siblings between them. Intermediary brothers and sisters, Anthony said, giggling, With us, it was him, a decade later, me.

I asked, Do you know if your parents tried having other children?

Smiling with embarrassment, Anthony said, I do not know and have not tried finding out. But, anyway, I do have a first memory of my brother. It might not be a true beginning-of-it-all first memory, maybe it's what I remember the strongest, but I must've been eight, almost nine, because he'd come back from boot camp and looked different. His edges were sharper. His physique was more defined. His jaws and especially his shoulders. They were, Anthony paused, raising clawed hands a foot above his own shoulders, Huge, so much bigger than they had been. But he carried himself differently, too, which is odd to say, I know, because I can't remember him strongly before then. He was different. That's the only word I can think of … And I was like, Wow, I have never seen this person. It's embarrassing to say, but I was awed. He was a man. The family had two men now. I wanted to be a man, too.

Anthony, at once, resembled the boy he'd been, his face relaxed and eyes awakened momentarily. I replied, How did you want to be a man?

He answered, Michael was in the Army, like our dad, that's one way. But, also, that—Anthony straightened his back, pushed forward his chest—that, that aura. You can sense it. Afterwards, I felt closer to him. Maybe closer to him because I wanted to be like him. We clearly didn't hang out. He was older and lived out of state, but I remember feeling more connected. It could have been just my admiration. He sent me stuff, though, trinkets, key chains, etcetera. And when Michael visited, we'd go places. Mostly, it was the entire family, but sometimes me and him.

And you wanted to be like him?

Yes.

I couldn't tell if Anthony had stopped to reflect or would not go further. How did you want to be like him?

Um, the service. Signing up was always somewhere in my head. I like to think it was more because of him than our dad. Especially not Uncle Bobby. I remember something my brother told me once. So, he was in the Army during the Gulf War. The first one.

But he never saw action and I remember him telling me how much he regretted not going over there. He really wanted to fight. He said something like, he didn't say he felt cheated, but something to the effect. With our family history—I was sixteen when that conversation happened, so Michael had been out of the service a few years. Ten years later, 9/11 and all that. I'm in college, but part of me is saying, You have to leave school and join. It was a possibility after high school—Who knows why I didn't? But now I have this war, these wars, and the opportunity is there. I couldn't, though. I never went to the recruiter's office. I passed by one frequently but never stepped in. But it's good I didn't, right? He stopped talking, then said, I was asking you … Can you imagine being in house-to-house combat? I've read a little about urban warfare and that shit is, you, it's, everything is on top of you. I think someone compared it to fighting in an escape room. Killing people, possibly being killed. Or worse. But, also, I think I should have—someplace inside me believes that.

Sorry, but we should stop. Let's pick up here next time. This is important.

OK, yeah, Anthony responded.

It was summer. He removed his over-the-shoulder bag from the coat rack and held it to his side like a school book. I opened the door, said, See you next time.

Have a good one, he answered, and turning to me without stopping, added with a grin, I wanted to be a Marine, like Uncle Bobby.

Michael married in his late-twenties, divorced in his mid-thirties, remarried in his early forties. A daughter from his first marriage was in college. A daughter from his current marriage was in grade school. He lived in Georgia, as he had the last fifteen years, working in the office of a construction firm. Relations with his family were good but disappointingly matter-of-fact. Anthony had told me this and also that Michael rarely returned more than once every other Christmas. Janie gave me his contact information, however. After our discussion, she emailed and said, They were close. Michael would know more about what Anthony was thinking than Hank or me. I pray he can help. Or you can help him. Michael won't tell us a thing. My response was noncommittal: I thanked her, wished her well, without saying if I'd reach out to him, though I undeniably would. As much as anyone, I wanted to know more than I did. Anthony's death had also shocked me.

He answered the phone, Yeah, as though we were business partners. I introduced myself, having called the exact time we'd scheduled. Michael responded, Yeah, I know. He either sounded like Anthony or I believed he did. I don't know what my mom was thinking, Michael continued, You talked to her and want to talk to me?

Not quite, I answered, Your mother asked to talk, which we did, and afterwards, she passed along your email address, believing we should speak.

About what? I don't know what happened. My parents are there, you're his therapist. I feel like I should be asking you.

You're completely justified to feel that way.

I bet, he muttered.

After hesitating, I responded, Let me start by thanking you for agreeing to meet with me. I know this has been difficult for you and your family. I waited for a reply, but Michael said nothing. So I continued, How was your relationship with Anthony?

Anthony killing himself isn't my fault. He's been like that since forever. And our relationship was fine.

I heard typing, and for a second, earnestly asked myself if Michael was transcribing our exchange. But I remembered he was at work, though apparently, without taking a break as I assumed he would. That Michael had not stopped and was able and content to toil away surprised then angered me. My image of Michael became what I imagined of Hank before meeting him, something monstruous, bullying, and unconcerned about others. I rocked back in my chair and grabbed my forehead. Across from me, next to the chair were clients sit, was a coffee table and I noticed the last person I saw had left a glass stain. They'd come in with a large coffee, the bottom of which dripped with spillage from a self-serve station. I was gazing at this dried, fragmentary circlet without moving or thinking to clean it.

Hello. Hello. Hello. Are you there?

Yes, I am. Sorry, I lost you for a moment.

Is there anything in particular you want to know for your work? I'm busy, and honestly, confused about a lot of what's going on.

To myself I said, I want to find a reasonable answer. I said to myself, Cause and effect are less important than a coherent picture. I said to myself, Have you ever seen a painting and grasped its totality without comprehending a brushstroke? I said to myself, That is the effect I want, to appreciate Anthony's life and death and feel more than confusion. I said to Michael, Understanding your and Anthony's relationship is important to understanding what happened. That's why I spoke with your parents and am speaking with you. I know—

Uh-huh. What to say about that? Anthony was my little brother. I loved him. Was I as welcoming as I should have been every second of our lives? No. But that's how it, we didn't really grow up together having the same experiences around the same times. Being a lot older made a difference. I can't say much more, I don't believe.

My head started to ache. I lost my place in our conversation.

But Michael kept talking: I'm not surprised, if that's what you really want to know. When mom called, I knew either Dad or Anthony had died. It was one of those phone calls. Not because of the time of day or whatever, I'm certain you know what I mean. I saw her name and thought, Dad or Anthony. I answered, and yep, Anthony.

Why weren't you surprised?

He just seemed like the kind of kid. I wasn't home with him growing up, but when I visited or saw him, it's hard to describe.

But, no, I wasn't surprised. I—even with him as an adult, that didn't change my mind. It, with Anthony, seemed possible and that's not true for most people. Sorry, I have to go. Stuff here is crazier than I expected.

Oh, OK. Thank you again.

Sure thing.

When I leave, occasionally, it's not every time, it's infrequent, but I have a real strong desire to hug you goodbye. I admit this as we're ending today—Don't worry, I won't hug you.

Anthony mentioned, in passing, his closest friend, Annie, whom he'd met in college. He called their bond immortal but generally spoke of her as if she were a suggestion in his life rather than a longtime buddy. I asked him, Tell me again, How long have you known her?

Not this, he responded, Twenty years about. You saw me trying to get away from that topic.

Not this, I jokingly said, tossing a hand in the air, Why not this?

Why? Because when she comes up, in here anyway, I also remember how we met, and I know what I'm supposed to do in therapy, say it all, but I also want to avoid getting into that episode.

I shook my head then Anthony cycled through looking at me and looking away. Finally, I responded, I don't understand.

We met in college. That's all I've told you. But more of the story is we met at the stadium. The football stadium. For a charity event.

OK, I said. While Anthony struggled to communicate what had been unspoken, I anticipated what he'd reveal: he and Annie had dated or hooked up and unresolved feelings complicated their lives. The classic simplicity of his conflict was a relief.

Anthony replied, It was raising money for—Do you remember that earthquake in Iran? Or was it Al-geria—Tunisia?

I don't.

Well, one of them, he responded, You know those fundraisers wherein you walk, climb stairs. They're held at the Hancock Center. But it was that type of thing. Maybe each death counted a step and you had to walk the casualties? Sounds grotesque. We met there. I don't know, we just ended up next to each other and started chatting. This campus has a massive football stadium with nothing else around, like a college on the moon. We, as I said, met, started talking, and walked together. But it became a competition between us. I was picking up my pace and she was going faster. Anthony leaned forward and pumped his arms, We were racing. She was more athletic than me—well, she has better stamina, not more athletic—which I can admit now, so I kinda slowed down first. We'd get together to exercise afterwards, a lot of similar activities. I keep picturing being back at the football stadium and doing the same thing, but that can't be right? Me and her in the stadium. We ran stairs other places, though. And hills. The topography is different there.

This became a thing between you?

A thing between us? Hill workouts? Or stairs, too? Yeah. That's what you mean, Thing between us?

Yes, I was referring to exercising together. Were you implying more?

You believe I'm hiding something, Anthony replied, I am but not what you think. Annie and I have never been together. That, he chuckled, would not be good. People assume we're lying, Anthony and Annie, but it's true. What I haven't said, though, is I kept pushing myself even when she wasn't around as a challenge. I'd exercise alone, what I'm talking about now mostly happened when I was alone, and run as hard as I could. To pass-out exhaustion.

Anthony broke off, hoping those details were sufficient. When he was most fearful and vulnerable, I was expected to intuit his needs and to know his thoughts, to ease his anxieties. I wanted to sit with him, support his attempt to continue in our silence, as he became more comfortable, gathered the courage to speak. During those episodes, however, he'd fill the atmosphere with such despair at my failure to meet expectations that I wanted to flee. But I couldn't leave and sitting in quietness was unbearable. I responded, Anthony, you know what I say, interpretation not divination. What's up? Let me know.

He lifted his eyes to that corner. OK. I'll just … The day I raced Annie, this hadn't happened before, while exercising, my heart was beating faster than ever and I started thinking, I might have a heart attack. But that made me want to go harder and faster. I was saying to myself, If I have heart attack or a stroke, whichever, but if I die exercising, that'd be OK. No one would suspect it was done on purpose. Especially with paramedics around. It felt like an—not easy, but acceptable or believable way to die. I didn't start working out more, but I did exercise to the point of, Damn, I can barely breathe or my chest is crazy heaving or my head's throbbing … Anthony lowered his eyes, looked near but not at me, then raised his hands as though crowning himself, Have you had a headache that wraps around, around your temples, your forehead, I can't remember what the back of your head is called, but around the entire thing, like a band is pressing against it and the top is going to blow off? When I see joggers or walk by a gym with those huge windows that let you see in, I wonder if anyone is doing that. I'm skeptical when I read stories about people just happening to have heart attacks while exercising, too. You can force it. It can be done, I think. HIIT jobs, he joked.

Anthony might have committed suicide. I acknowledged that possibility under the influence of others. His family didn't know him best, but they knew him well enough to be taken with absolute seriousness. They'd loved him since birth. I don't claim to have known Anthony better, but our relationship was unlike theirs. We met in adulthood and the person I knew experienced depression, was at times morbid, but had never tried to kill himself. Thinking of death and wanting to die are not the same. My perspective differed from his family's because they saw him in ways I could not and I knew details about him they did not. Had we viewed Anthony's passing similarly, I might have stopped without seeking more details about his life. But the incongruence helped tug me where I wanted to go. I'd been disoriented personally and professionally by Anthony dying and needed to be placed upright. Whatever threshold existed, I'd likely crossed and was no longer behaving like a concerned therapist but a mourning intimate. I understood the risks and continued. If, at the end, I could explain, grasp an interpretation of, his death, I told myself, it would be shared with those who loved him. That promise was sincere and a way to defend myself from guilt and self-doubt.

I didn't have her last name, that of her business, and she had a first name as common as Annie in a world as large as ours. But what I knew plus college plus hometown plus Nashville were sufficient. I'd expected a long and possibly futile search, but this Annie was the only person Google suggested. Other than an out-of-place Flowering Dogwood, the images in my results were also of her and her decadent cookies. Annie's creations were pastel-colored, sprinkled and sugared, gussied up, lit, and photographed like tiny exotic dancers. She was a slender woman with small features and pointy ears and I suspected in person she was petite and energetic. Anthony's jokey description of her, Midwesterner turned Southern apostle, wasn't his offhand invention, as I thought, but a tagline Annie used on her website. On the about page was a picture of Annie and her kids, a girl and a boy, at a kitchen island with a large bowl, ingredients, and baking equipment in front of them. Smiling, their hands were covered with flour and dough. She had created this business for herself as well as her children, the page said. In the past, she'd been, Too focused on what didn't matter, but she decided, To chase her dreams. I clicked away, scrolling through her offerings, before returning to that page. Annie's skepticism of the South fell away and reemerged as love during college. Her encounter with its people and culture falsified her expectations. After graduating, she briefly returned to Michigan before moving to Florida, Virginia, finally Tennessee, where she met her husband at a food-and-beverage conference. He shared a birthday with her grandfather. Anthony had told me nothing about Annie—not even her full name, Anastasia.

I needed days to compose just a few lines. Expressing myself in writing had been effortless since childhood, but finding these desired words, getting their tone and order correct was undoable. Perhaps, she knew as little of my existence as I knew of hers. I was not a family member or friend. The grief we shared did not have an obvious connection, so an inexact phrase might not receive Annie's benefit of doubt. Nor could I allow myself to write and rewrite endlessly, which the most insecure and fearful parts of me wanted. I gathered bits of unfinished sentiments into a five-sentence whole but continued fighting uncertainty. After rereading my salutation, Dear Annie, I paused, unsure if I should use the name by which she'd been introduced to me or Anastasia. No, I told myself, No, and kept Annie then read until the end, through my condolences, saying who I was, and why I wanted to speak with her. I had planned to DM her on Facebook, via her business' page, when I noticed she also had a personal account. Her most recent posts were from September. She wrote, Make sure the people you love KNOW IT!!!!!

Minutes later, Devasted no words

Minutes after that, My best friend since college died. I don't want to believe it's real. Somebody wake me up from this!

Later that day, PLEASE PLEASE PLEASE TELL THE PEOPLE YOU LOVE I LOVE YOU. TELL THEM EVERY CHANCE YOU GET. EVERY DAY. LIFE IS PRECIOUS LIFE IS SHORT!

After four days, Annie posted, The world right now feels like a different place. I remember meeting Anthony and he looked so young. I thought he might break just standing there by himself. I don't know who said it but somebody said always talk to strangers. They were right! You don't know who you might meet! We went from not knowing each other at all to tight in one afternoon. You don't know someone then you can't imagine life without them. This person was a stranger and then you're going to know them forever. My heart's breaking writing these words. Thinking about all those times. Some of the memories at least make me smile. Anthony couldn't do a cartwheel. and nobody could teach him. He couldn't get his legs over. I saw him run miles and playing all kinds of sports but he couldn't do a cartwheel. I think he was afraid! He gave me a fake coupon to be cryogenically frozen when I turned 30! I still have it too! That's who Anthony was. He had something special for every person. My kids got birthday gifts from him every year and I remember one time something he sent got delayed in the mail and he was so angry because he thought it might look like he forgot. So much more I can say about him. I texted him the day he died and am so glad I did because at least I got to have a last moment with him. He wanted to switch places with me because the weather was so bad that he couldn't go for a walk. I said to him Anthony you don't like the south and he said I know but the weather is better. I wish I could go back and just tell him trust your instincts! It's too late before you realize, life is shorter than you think!!! You are loved and missed Anthony!

I don't keep a diary.

Why not?

Well, Anthony said, hearing the joke in his head and smirking, I think about it but I remember you're noting what's being said. The important stuff anyway. I kept a journal as a kid, though. Really.

I laughed, Of course.

Phil died early morning, August 11, 2020. Because he was alone, it'll never be certain how, but everyone, including me, believes he fell asleep while driving. No drugs, no alcohol. His car, going about forty miles an hour, crashed into a storefront. Before going to Portugal, I had not taken a day off in more than a year. I honored major holidays but saw clients on weekends. What's hard to fathom, increasingly so as days pass, is the time since his death already exceeds the length of our relationship. But that, perhaps, only proves the proverb, One recalls a flash of lightening more readily than the storm.

He and I liked to say we nearly met on an app, because a friend of mine and a friend of his, whose connection started online, convinced us to go out. Our first date was the Monday before Christmas and he arrived a tad less punctually than me, an inside joke I like to repeat. I chose a seat facing the café's entrance and its large windows overlooking the intersection. Minutes before meeting somebody, when any person arriving could be the one you're waiting for, I start to feel unease. I worry about forgetting a face I've never seen in person. I worry someone will enter and recognize me as I turn from their greeting. Phil's arrival was clear, however, although he wore a carmine skull cap pulled to his eyes and a bulky, faux-fur hood on his head. He flipped the hood back and extending from the fold of his cap was the bend of a green-striped peppermint stick. Forgetting the candy cane was there, Phil took off the beanie, snatching it from the top, and nearly caught the falling sweet in his left hand. The peppermint fell closer to me, but he was quicker to grab it. Rather than bending at the knees, Phil placed a hand on the table and leaned forward at the waist, a leg rising behind him. He sat and apologized for what happened. A mustache circled his lips toward the dimple in his chin, still noticeable beneath a two-day beard. Phil's eyes were brown, his hair tapered along the sides and larger, taller on top than I imagined, which he deftly finger-picked into style. No problem whatsoever, I said, Hopefully, it didn't break. Phil took off his coat and quickly fiddled with the candy before sliding it into the chest pocket of his light blue scrubs. The fall had cracked his peppermint midway up its spine. Well, good thing there's not a shortage, he joked. Phil smiled with a frown in his eyes, like a person uncertain how you'll react. I slid the menu to his side of the table.

Oh, boy, Phil said, I don't trust, Traditional, no. Traditional Japanese sencha. Nope.

Beg your pardon? I'd heard every word but wanted confirmation.

Phil answered, These teas, the menu says, Traditional. I was getting coffee anyway but … He sniggered.

I asked myself why a friend had set me up with this type of person. Moreover, she apparently adored a man who considered this guy a friend.

Phil looked up, I should tell you something right now, before we go any further: there are some labels I never trust: authentic, traditional, classic, rustic … earnest! He was giggling, If that's not something you can handle, well, offering a hand for me to shake, It's been a pleasure.

I smiled and answered, Oh, god.

Seriously, he continued. Another one, another one: Holy.

What? I laughed.

Holy Bible. Is, Holy, part of the official title or is it an advertising thing? Holy: that's the least trustworthy one!

I was smiling and laughing, You're an idiot, I told him.

Crazy like a fox. Phil, grinning drearily, tapped his head with an index finger.

That evening I nicknamed him Saint Authenticus. When I asked how to say authentic in Latin, he reached for his phone as if he'd been waiting for my signal. After a few minutes of scrolling and typing, a couple of false discoveries, he yelled, Authenticus!

May our victuals be nourishing, I said. He signed himself then reached to lay a hand on my head, but I grabbed it, You're—I don't know what to call you.

Phil had studied economics in college and spent the summer afterward loading UPS trucks and recording a rap album. Like many young people, he was responsible and imaginative, doing enough to find a so-called professional job while secretly longing to be forced another direction. In Phil's case, he also set an end-of-August deadline for himself. If no *good* jobs had been offered by the thirty-first, he'd commit to music. That happened on the twenty-eighth, close enough for disappointment but not close enough to be taken aback, so for almost twenty years he drafted esoteric, jargony memos and reports at various firms. The debut album of Mr. Phil, as he called himself, tentatively titled Philip I, was revisited during those years but remained unfinished. We shared this encounter with life, though I luckily pursued therapy in my late-twenties after selling insurance. So you understand, he told me. Phil had recently become a nurse and his next shift began hours after the café closed. I could walk you home and back without being late, he said.

I had a lot of fun.

Me too. It was a great night, he replied.

Phil was about five-nine, round and wide, his torso firm as ripening avocado. I stepped closer and made the sign of Christ on him. We embraced. He could have kissed me goodnight but didn't. Midway up the stairs I stopped to wave, and though I couldn't read his lips, mouthed in response, OK, I will.

When I called Anthony to the office, he looked up from his lap with eyebrows raised, but he didn't appear upset or overwhelmed. It was an expression, I thought, of someone who's forgotten a birthday or been reminded of a years-old, minor embarrassment.

I'm certain, he said, his face now relaxed, Certain. I don't use the word certain a lot, but someone was finishing a first date before coming inside. I suspect to a therapist office because there's so many here.

What makes you sure?

You didn't repeat, Certain. Well, if you put a gun to my forehead, I couldn't say no-doubt-one-hundred-thousand-percent certain, yes, it was a first date, but everything about their interaction said first date. I didn't see beginning to end, they were standing outside when I arrived. She came in right after me. I pushed the revolving door with my shoulder, to the side, leaning on it, and saw her walking up.

You do seem certain—

I am.

Why?

Everyone knows what a first-date ending looks like. Good first dates, bad first dates, whatever first dates. They're different but all their endings are recognizable.

And what happened now was?

A good one. I think. Not bad, unless they're great actors. It reminded me of my first date with Rachel. That's what I wanted to get to: our first date ended outside this building. She walked me here, how long …? Three years ago. -Ish. About the same general time I started seeing you.

I remember when you met and started going out, but I didn't know your first date ended outside. I thought you went to Millennium Park?

Yep, right before a session.

Was that planned?

He smiled, No. Why roll from one right into the other? I anticipated some distance between our date and our session. She cancelled. Not cancelled, but she changed where we'd meet. Very close to when we were supposed to get together actually. I was irked, but it wasn't a dealbreaker or some unforgiveable, just felt people are unpredictable: it's one date: keep pushing: see what happens. Anthony's eyebrows rose toward his hairline and that peculiar portrait hung on his face two or three seconds. We met online and I remember being surprised when we matched because when I saw her profile I thought, We'd probably do well in person, but I don't know if that's evident on an app. I'd seen her before, too. But she and I had a short back and forth then decided to meet in person. I suppose we don't waste much time before committing to each other. So, we were supposed to go to one place, that McDonald's a few blocks from here, which is important, but minutes, I mean, this was practically as I'm leaving, she texted me to meet her at Foster Beach. I said I couldn't because of an appointment and she said, OK, how about Millennium Park? and I said, Sure. I was annoyed, though. But I get there and find her and jutting out of her backpack are two lacrosse sticks. We walk around and she takes them out and we start tossing a ball back and forth. I was terrible because I'd never played lacrosse, but she said, I had to play today! But it was fun. She had a ton of shit in her backpack, too. A remote-controlled plane, I remember. Then she walked with me here, and even though we'd been talking, right outside the conversation was going, like going-going, I thought she didn't want me to leave. Eventually, though, I said, I have to go or she'll, referring to you, start without me, which made her laugh. But that McDonald's, where we planned to meet, she and I had been there at the same time well before we connected. Anthony became agitated, his voice rose, opening his arms and flashing upwards his palms, he said accusatorily, insecurely: I've told this story before?

He had and I answered, Go ahead.

This was months before I saw her profile or we met in person. I know it was definitely her, though. I'm certain. She was waiting for a date. Because, like I said, you know how these situations look. It's easy when someone is waiting for another person, especially if it's a date. It's different. So, she's waiting, checking the time, looking around, slyly not trying to be seen looking around, but no one comes. At some point, she orders food, at some point, sits down, but she goes back to the counter, gets a bag for it, and leaves. Whoever it was stood her up. I told Rachel this, maybe months after we'd started going out, we were already living together, and she denied it. Not having been to that Mickey D's but being stood up and that I saw it, but I know what happened. Now, her position is it could have happened, as in, I might have seen her stood up. She finally acknowledges being stood up, but I can't tell if she's admitting I witnessed it or if she's acquiesced that I won't change my mind. Does she believe she told me but watching it is in my head? I'm going to sound like a misogynist when I say this, but embarrassment could be the reason. An attractive woman being stood up has to cut, and I can't imagine whomever she was waiting for was as good looking as her. I don't believe she is, or was, trying to gaslight me. Not purposefully. But it's odd how long she resisted before admitting that itty amount. His body motionless, Anthony's eyes patrolled the room, planlessly circling and darting.

Then he stopped, raised his eyebrows again, but with a half-hearted smile. Some things can be said but not explained, he continued, and I bet she feels the same about me.

The call was from an unknown person with an unfamiliar area code. They also left a voicemail, which I played expecting to delete moments after it began. Hello, she said, and in the fractions of seconds before her next words, I thought, Rachel. She continued, This is Rachel, Anthony Glass's partner. I—Anthony gave me your number. Years ago now. I'm sorry for calling unexpectedly, but … Rachel was silent. I thought she might hang up. … I needed to talk to you. There's no other or better way to describe what I'm doing. I want to talk. Again, this is Rachel, Anthony's partner. Please, give me a call back. I had not heard her speak before, yet after a few syllables, I was thinking of her as, Rach', as Anthony often said. I returned her call, during which she sounded more certain. It was if her initial attempt to reach me had been a dry run she accidentally carried out. Regardless, over a five- or six-minute conversation, we agreed to meet at a café near where she and Anthony lived.

The second Sunday in December, hours before our appointment, Rachel asked if I could come to their apartment instead. When I arrived at the building, she was standing outside in green corduroys, an overlarge red button-up shirt with green stripes, an arm folded over her stomach, and alternately drinking from a large cup of coffee and watching puffs of breath rise into the air. Despite it being my first time seeing Rachel, I knew this was her. If I'd known nothing more, her style of dress hinted Anthony. Even so, she did not recognize me. Rachel glanced and smiled a tiny bit, as you would to discourage a street vendor, but I didn't veer away and she looked again but closer and more intently. Margaret? She transferred the mug to her left hand and embraced me with her right arm. I'm so happy you could make it, Rachel said, And sorry for the last-minute change. Much of her black hair was tied imperfectly to the back, she had dark eyes, and as I thought to myself, movie-star cheeks. I recalled how Anthony had once described her, … resembles Penelope Cruz a little, but a normal, white version.

Follow me, Rachel said, leading seven or eight steps from sidewalk's edge to building. Her pant hems were upturned and secured with safety pins.

It was a second-floor apartment where she and Anthony had moved months after they met. The walk to their front door was speechless. Once inside, she finished her coffee and grabbed a coat from a nearby rack. I completely whiffed putting it on before going out, she said, Now, I'm freezing.

I reflexively apologized for having made her wait.

You didn't make me, she responded, I like greeting people outside. Finding the building, buzzing the right door can be confusing. Would you like something to drink?

I hung up my coat and noticed on the wall a bright red pillowcase into which had been sewn tiny, varicolored letters and boomerangs along with the sentence, Letters are boomerangs that always return.

Before I answered, Rachel, moving into another room, continued, Coffee? Tea? Water? I have juice, too. Orange juice.

Just water, thanks. I walked further inside, following the apartment's layout. It resembled an art studio more than a place where people lived. Different-sized easels, paints, ink pens, pictures and frames, books, yarns, fabrics, desks, maps, plants, at least three cameras, and in one corner a bird cage with a drinking bird toy inside. Rachel reemerged holding an empty glass.

I forget to ask if you wanted filtered or tap?

Tap is OK.

Great!

I kept walking slowly and perusing. When Rachel came back holding glasses of water, I was leafing through images cut from junk mailers that were on a dining room table. I don't know what I'm going to do with those yet, she said, But they were so weird I had to keep them. She handed me a glass and cleared a section of the table with a forearm, revealing two coasters. We sat and she said, Wow, you're here. I would not have expected to meet you three months ago. I can say this: I was somewhat jealous of you. I know that's ridiculous but … We communicated really well. Anthony was my best friend. But the, the existence of someone, another woman, he could confide in. I know: stupid, right? You were his therapist, not another woman.

No, no, it isn't, I told her, That's not unusual. Partners often have those feelings. It happens frequently.

Rachel's face briefly shimmered as if she'd seen a birthday cake instants before hearing, Surprise! That's not what I wanted to talk about, she said, then speaking to herself, What did I want to talk about? Not this but … She went to a wall shelf and returned with a framed five-dollar bill. Handing it to me, Rachel said: After Anthony and I's first date, I found this on a sidewalk downtown. It was face up, too. I was in front of that Block-food-hall place. I saw it and looked around, like, Is this a setup? Does anyone else see it? But then I thought, Maybe it's a sign? And it was face up. I didn't know if, for sure, it was a sign until later.

When did you know?

Soon. We talked more that evening. Texted. Oh, I walked him to see you I remember. He said you would start without him! I was thinking about that and laughing when I found the five-dollar bill. I had this picture in my head—even though I didn't know who you were, your name—of a therapist listening and nodding to an empty chair. Real serious, too. We laughed and Rachel got up again. In the corner, beneath stacks of books, was a mahogany desk with ornate, silvery handles and scuffs marks on its sides that appeared to be from the 1950s. She opened the middle drawer, which meekly resisted her tug, and removed a folded, azure hand towel. Rachel sat, moved aside her glass and coaster, the framed bill, and carefully undid the folds. Inside was a collection of three Moleskin notebooks: colored Brisk Blue, Cranberry Red, and Myrtle Green. Anthony and I, she said, were going to write a movie longhand. Well, initially, we planned to use the typewriter, but we never bought ribbon. Rachel looked at a corner behind me. I turned and saw, atop a small cabinet equally as old timey and scuffed as that desk, a shut, maroon typewriter case.

I didn't know you could still buy ribbon.

You can find it. We hadn't come up with an idea, she smirked, but writing a movie is something both of us wanted to do. But one day, when we were out, we decided to get these, figuring longhand might be better because we could see each other's handwriting and it would feel even more collaborative. Yeah, but, we didn't start. We only ripped out a couple of pages from this one, Rachel continued, holding the blue notebook, to play Word of Damocles. You know about this, the word game Anthony invented?

I didn't know Anthony invented a word game, I replied, How's it played?

It's awesome! One second. She paused, attentively refolded the Moleskins inside the towel, and returned them to their drawer. As she moved from that desk to the typewriter's cabinet, where she opened another middle drawer, Rachel said, It's really fun—and challenging. She turned around holding a little stack of notebook paper, You pick two letters, any two letters—or it could be three or four but we seldom used more than two—and you set a timer and try to write as many words as you can that start with those letters. She stopped walking and said, Sorry, do you want to? I got excited and took for granted …

Definitely, I told her, It sounds fun.

OK, she replied, handing me sheets of paper. She lifted away some of those on the table and found two ink pens. You get a point per syllable, Rachel continued, And you can double-up, so for instance, writing see and seer is fine. Putting her phone on the table, We usually did two or three minutes, depending on our mood, what do you think? Is three too long?

No, that's not too long.

Great. Your choice. Which letters?

A-M, I answered quickly.

Ready, go.

A-M: amnesty, amnesia, ammo, ammunition, among, amorphous, ample, amplify, ambivalent, ambivert … Let's alternate, I told her, You choose the next set.

I-S.

I-S: is, isomorphic, isomorphism, isolate, isolated, isolation, isolationism, islet …

T-A.

T-A: talk, take, tableau, tar, tandem, tact, task, taboo, tacit, tactical, tactful, tag …

K-E.

K-E: kernel, key, kempt, keep, keeper, keepsake, keyhole, keynote, keyboard, keyway, keystroke …

B-Y.

B-Y: bye, bye-bye, bygone, bypass, byproduct, Byzantine, bye-and-bye, bystander, byte …

M-E.

M-E: mercy, merge, merciful, merciless, meridian, mere, meter, merchant, mental, mentality, mentalist, menu, meow, merengue
…

I asked Rachel if I could keep the sheets on which I had written my words. While we played and during our chat afterwards, I feared they'd be thrown out but blenched at my need rather than fear of her response. My question waited until I had put on my coat and was standing at the door.

Please do, Rachel said, grasping my hands like a grandmother and hurrying to the table to retrieve them. I watched her from behind, gathering my sheets of paper then momentarily go to another room. She reappeared with a manila envelope. I put them in here, Rachel told me, It was wonderful to meet you.

It was wonderful to meet you, too, I replied, and we hugged.

Rachel twisted a deadbolt that hadn't been locked and her hand fell slowly to the knob. I heard the cock when she turned it but the door did not open. When Rachel started speaking, her head and eyes were angled toward the floor. The person who'd left that voicemail returned. I know what Anthony's family believes, she said, They practically think he jumped into the lake. She grasped one of my hands, Anthony didn't kill himself. He didn't. I know he didn't. He could get sad. Some of that was natural. In one of his profile pictures, I remember him looking more depressed than his smile. Partly upbringing. It's who he was, but look around, everyone is a little sad now. That made it worse for him, but he didn't kill himself. I would know. I can't say how but I would. We were connected.

I held tighter her hand. She held tighter mine.

I had an insane dream last night.
Really?
But I can't remember any of it.

Instead of sitting, as he has since starting therapy, Anthony lies on the couch. He lets himself in (I don't move, not even to acknowledge his entrance), shuts the door, and as if it is utterly, unremarkably normal, pillows his interlaced fingers under his head. Anthony appears taller lying down. He wants me to acknowledge the change first, he wants—Oh, he's talking. Perhaps he's been talking since lying down. His lips are moving, but I can't hear him. Perhaps he's been talking since his arrival.

Louder, please, Anthony, I say.
Anthony, I say again, louder, please, I cannot hear you.
Anthony, sorry to interrupt, but can you speak up a tad?
Anthony.
Anthony.
Hmph.
I think to myself, A comfortable man is a talkative man. That's the adage? I say to him, Anthony, please, speak louder.
Hmph again.
Now I get up and slowly move to him, bent over at the waist

as though I'm being led by a drip-drip-drip-drip-drip to the couch. I'm standing next to him, over him in fact, but cannot hear what's being said. His lips are going faster, more consistently than they ever had when speaking audibly. Why am I not angry? I notice something and ask, Anthony, do you see that cobalt-blue haze in the air? Hmmm. More unusualness. I can only manage one oddity at once. I go to my knees and turn my right ear toward him and lean in. I'm eavesdropping on a person who's talking inches from my ear. Breath is present, but yes, because he's breathing. But is he talking? I tell him, Get up, Anthony. Get up, and I take him by the arm. Sit there, I say, directing him to The Chair. He sits and I lie down.

Co 27, I say, is the chemical element for cobalt, but Co is also the abbreviation for company. I sit up and look over my shoulder. He's no longer talking but eying me attentively. I think he's listening, but it's difficult to know from this position. I lie down. Twenty-seven is different, I continue, Two and seven is nine, but two times seven is fourteen and seven minus two is five and seven divided by two is three and a half. That's all understandable.

We switch places.

Anthony talks and, once more, is also silent. I listen. On my knees again with an ear nearly at his lips, I listen. I return to The Chair and listen.

We switch places.

I talk.

He listens.

We switch places.

He talks.

I listen.

We switch places.

I talk.

He listens.

We switch places.

He talks.

I listen.

We switch places.

I talk.

He listens.

The session ends. We are standing face to face. I say, See you next time, as his lips also move (I intuit it's also, See you next time), and we both try to sit in The Chair. We laugh a madcap, lunatic laughter, with heads swiveling and arms flailing, then regaining our calm, offer each other the seat. Or, excuse me, The Seat.

Danke schön, he says. Audible speech! His words are clear! Understandable! Obvious as the less attractive twin!

But I don't speak German and neither does Anthony. Nevertheless, I respond, Bitte schön.

He leaves.

I take The Chair.

When I opened the consulting room's door, Anthony raised his head just enough to convey situational awareness. He dragged himself toward and past me, re-lowering his face with every sunless footstep. And that fugacious, soundless interaction was enough to affect me. I was immediately saddened.

Anthony said little and what he said was incomplete. He would blurt complaints about a coworker, undelivered mail, or another irritant then withdraw into angry, folded-arms muteness. His fight was internal, however, not with me, though he refused all my attempts to help. I don't have much to say, Anthony would tell me, or, I'm trying, but I'm not capable of doing what I'm not capable of doing. In different forms and ways, I continued asking, What do you want to say? and he, becoming less subtle with each reply, maintained, Nothing. I want to say what I'm saying. I wasn't angry with him, but my emotional state risked being as despondent as his. That, as much as my failure to open him up, is why I stopped talking. I could not want this more than him. We sat without exchanging a word and essentially motionless, except that Anthony would intermittently glimpse to see if I were still present. I was.

Forty minutes passed and Anthony pressed his elbows against the chair's arms to lift himself and sit more erectly. He had done so abruptly and noisier than necessary. I thought and wished that was prelude to him speaking, but Anthony, now stretching his wrists flexors, kept silent. I readjusted, raising a hand to cup my jawline. He said,

I hate when people compare me to Uncle Bobby. Do you know how it feels to be compared with somebody you've never met? It's infuriating. My parents do it. Michael will do it and he was a kid when Uncle Bobby shot his fucking head off! I was having a good day. I thought I was having a good day and I start talking to my mom. I said something about being annoyed with the principal at my school. He'll talk to you sometimes while he's tapping a pen in the palm of his hand. It's fucking annoying, especially when he's supposedly telling you something important. That happened a few days ago, but I was talking to my mom about it—I don't know, making conversation—and she says, You sound just like Bobby. Stuff like that got to him, too. Why would you say a thing like that to me? Why? My whole life they've been doing that: This reminds me of Bobby. Oh, what you're doing reminds me of Bobby. You look exactly like Bobby. I've seen pictures of him, and yeah, I get the resemblance. A little bit. Anybody can tell we're related. But he and my dad resemble each other, too, and Michael, too. Maybe me and Bobby a little more but whatever. It's infuriating. I don't know anything about him but that he always kept to himself. That's how people in my family describe it: he kept to himself. Everything I've heard about him makes me think he was depressed. He did kill himself, so … When I keep being compared to him, I'm just, I don't know. What to do. They don't understand what that all means. It's not a harmless little opinion. A harmless family factoid. It has meaning—for me although maybe not for them. Is this a stupid thing to believe, it might be, but when I get compared to Uncle Bobby, it feels predictive. It feels, to me, you know, like almost, like they're seeing the future but also creating the future. Make sense? I don't know. You know me, what I deal with, I,

I, I don't know. I don't—I have moments, but I don't want to end up like Uncle Bobby. But I ask myself, What do they know that I don't? I can't pretend to have complete awareness, sometimes people know you better than you know yourself. Rach' gets me in ways that make me think, Damn, I wasn't going to figure that out. You, too. You understand me differently, so maybe my family does also. They knew me before I knew I was alive. When I was a little flesh sack of energy. Can you know how someone is going to turn out in life? Maybe? Dad says Bobby was never different, i.e., he wasn't totally surprised when Bobby killed himself. That could be rationalization, though. I wonder if he's trying to make himself feel better by believing it was going to happen regardless. If someone wants to commit suicide, there's not a lot you can do. But Dad might be telling himself, Hank, you couldn't have done more. This … Uncle Bobby.

Anthony wept, reluctantly then without shame, looked into that corner and repeated, Uncle Bobby, before muttering dismissively, I'm like Uncle Bobby.

I was becoming tearful but had yet to cry. I'm sorry, I said to Anthony, But we have to pause here.

The Last Dictator

Part I

1

Oliver Apple, a stage name, the first an homage to Sir Laurence and the last an homage to New York City, often thought of his past. Had he been asked why, Oliver would have replied, "Given the time I spend with myself, I'd be happy to think of something else," but no one ever asked him (or wondered what he daydreamed about), and regardless, he was neither repressed nor uncreative enough to quit a memory. Driving a thought away seemed to him masochistic, violence done to imagination, and that he'd failed to live the life of an artist, which in middle-age, Oliver still envisioned a bohemian existence of artmaking and self-indulgence, gave his recollections and fantasies more importance. His psychic world was ever-vibrant even when the material world called him away. He remembered being twelve years old. He remembered Mrs. Morell and how she would stop mid-sentence to mention the beauty of a Robin or to guess the path of a plane overhead as if emanating from her mouth had made all thoughts related. She, Oliver recalled, appeared younger than his parents—Mrs. Morell was then, as a matter of fact, one and a half decades younger than he was now— and it was Mrs. Morell who introduced him to adulthood. Not by taking his virginity, no, definitely not, though he remembered sunburned legs extending beyond the hem of her skirts when she knelt beside him, and perhaps not unrelatedly, that around this period, too, were his earliest fears of being called to the front of the classroom with an erection. Along with everything else she did, Mrs. Morell administered a career assessment, a set of well-meaning, multiple-choice questions, designed to give students a good idea as to whether dreams and potential were a match. A certain type of person, the fully grown pessimist and know-it-all, the type who designs tests and drafts contracts, can't fathom that a wrong choice can also knock life's dominos in the direction of happiness, but from the disappointment of adults often comes the suffering of children. To "properly" measure suitability, students listed their dream jobs beforehand, and Mrs. Morell, who was aware of the sham, nevertheless did her work, asking them one by one, "What do you want to be when you grow up?" Oliver was sure of himself. He answered, "A thespian," a word he'd recently learned and more recently learned to pronounce.

Mrs. Morell offered a mundane synonym, "Actor?" to make sure Oliver wasn't mistaken.

"Yes," Oliver reiterated slowly, careful not to botch his second time saying the word, "a thespian."

Mrs. Morell replied, "Okay," and with slender, champagne-pink fingers swiftly typed next to his name, a-c-t-o-r, index then middle and ring and pinkie then middle again, before standing and encircling Oliver, bringing her left hand to the keyboard: /t-h-e-s-p-i-a-n (less convinced of the test makers' intellect than they were of the children's). That's what Oliver remembered: the first time he told an adult outside his family what he dreamed of becoming. Doing so made him feel grown up, as if one became an adult through certainty, and twenty-eight years later, in spite of what he'd learned in his actual adulthood, remembering that ancestor to himself still warmed his body from nipples to navel, evoked the sensation of recovering an heirloom that was never far away.

Not that it matters to the storyteller, but as often happens when someone's reminiscing, a few details of Oliver's account were wrong. That he took a career assessment at twelve years old and declared his life's dream for the first time was correct, but Mrs. Morell was not the person who proctored the exam nor was it taken in her classroom. He and his classmates had been shuffled to a computer lab where Mrs. Morell handed them to Mrs. Moller (who, it is true, would be Oliver's Spanish teacher a year later). Mrs. Moller was as old then as he was now and resembled her younger colleague solely in the transposed memories of Oliver Apple. Mrs. Moller's hair was long and black with ends flipped in a retro style, the smell of which revealed a love of cigars, while Mrs. Morell's hair was shorter with a pattern of loose curls and a scent of lilac conditioner. The older woman had dark eyes, was thin, but the younger's eyes were a shade of green (which twelve-year-old Oliver thought exotic) and she was fuller in form. Mrs. Moller gathered responses to "What do you want to be when you grow up?" and typed "actor/thespian" next to his name, as unimpressed with the test makers as Mrs. Morell certainly would have been, yet it was Mrs. Morell who in a different context, some other day responded "Actor?" when Oliver said he wanted to be a thespian.

We could, if it were not just intriguing but necessary, focus more on this case of the remembered and the provable—also conveniently eluding his memory were the results—but such fantasies are numerous in life and hereabout is where Oliver usually paused, too. From these mix-and-match memories everything moved undisturbed between past and present, which brings us, briefly at least, to the here and now. His, and transitively our, location in space-time is an autumnal weekday, October specifically, about 1700 hours. Though Oliver has a poor view from his desk, there's a bittersweet half-light on the horizon, beams of which nevertheless muscled into the lobby where he sat, so that when Oliver looked up from his daydream, he saw an hallucinogenic shade of red coating every surface. His uniform is a predictable white shirt with black shoes, black tie, and black pants. Unlike his colleagues, however, each day Oliver waged a small war against conformity with a pair of loud socks (today was orange) and lately preferred wearing skinny ties because they accentuated a naturally stout torso. His upper body, from which hung a pair of equally blockish and hairy arms, was also recently less fat—rather than not fat at all—since Oliver rededicated himself to fitness. It was a career move with health and, he believed, obvious aesthetic benefits, which is why he often took off his work blazer. This bulk ended with an ass his former wife called enormous before tapering into absurdly slim legs and small feet, neither of which appeared sufficient to carry his top half, but he'd successfully returned to the thickset phase he occupied between the birth of his daughter and his daughter's first birthday. Good enough. His head was another issue. Large, too, Oliver wasn't bald though hints of balding were clear, but an upcoming (and because of these signs of aging, urgent) project meant he couldn't preemptively shave his head. But, whether he knew it or not, this was better for him: with a shaved head, his small, dark brown eyes, relatively large lips and cheeks, he'd resemble an out-of-work authoritarian.

The lobby was decorated with two couches, one blue and one red, a marble coffee table between them with fiddle-leaf figs and birds of paradise dotting spaces along a wall nearby. On the lobby's opposite side hung a rectangular mirror in which the plants could see their reflections and behind that partition was a mailroom whose surfaces glittered with silver-plated affluence. The front door was glass as were the panels of the vestibule onto which it opened and the second door that finally led to the lobby. At the front desk, Oliver could see it all: people as they walked by the building's floor-to-ceiling windows, and residents, guests, and deliverymen who entered and departed. Moreover, what could not be seen in front of him, Oliver witnessed on security cameras. He often scrolled through angles of observation, accessing views of different areas to fight boredom and perhaps luck into seeing something memorable—filling his two monitors, for instance, with scenes of the lobby, then switching to an incalculable number of hallways, then randomly chosen alleys, then areas of the parking garage, traveling wherever mood escorted him.

Oliver had been relatively more successful staying engaged than witnessing the unforgettable, unless you consider watching drunks vomiting and brawling on late-night sidewalks or couples making out on squares of street-lit pavement indelible. Occasionally, he also followed people from their condos into the elevator, eyeing them to their first floor arrival, and through the lobby and outside until they were no longer visible, shifting the camera he watched with every change of location. But surveillance was one of many perks. Residents also treated him warmly and he always worked holidays. Oliver had been at Happy Gardens since it opened—his fifteen years longer than many of the condo owners—and quickly appreciated being at the front desk during national celebrations, such that whenever a coworker with less seniority asked why he didn't take off, Oliver would deflect with a tender-hearted platitude such as, "I don't mind working these days and letting you all have time with your families." In reality, he received food on Memorial Day, while being frequently mistaken for a veteran, and the Fourth of July was wonderful—he watched fireworks via rooftop cameras—and happily remembered eating a buffet of homemade barbecue before starting his diet, though Labor Day the year prior was the last on which he gorged with cakes (the month before he gave away every slice except chocolate). But all the food wasn't tasty—desserts, which many tried and few conquered, in particular. Helen Dipper, an attorney on the seventeenth floor, stood out in this regard. She especially liked baking cobblers, but concentrated too much on perfecting her fruits and not enough on saving her soggy crusts. Nevertheless, she was born and raised in Portland, Oregon, so Oliver didn't criticize her for blundering the forte of the South and Midwest. And, besides, those festivities were prologue to the holiday season. November through December was the period when, as Oliver joked, "I never have to buy groceries," and more importantly, residents tipped him for a year of being good-mannered and smiling in their presence. Between the fourth Thursday of November and the first week of January, Oliver would collect a couple thousand untaxed dollars, which was enough to treat himself with a new phone or high-priced sneakers. Yet, Oliver was disgusted by how the tips were given to him. They weren't gifted directly, honestly, hand to hand in the open, but furtively, as if the prohibition against talking religion and money extended to hiding cash and checks in Christmas cards that were then placed in nondescript envelopes. Nothing was as natural, as appropriate as the exchange of money for work, and the people who lived in Happy Gardens must've understood this, so why the shamefaced behavior? Another of Oliver's counterfactuals: he was as rich and well-connected as the wealthiest resident in the building and carried himself with the pride of a dozen Caesars.

He smiled without exposing a tooth, raised his chin, then added, "Have a nice evening, Mr. Jackson."

Through a door to his right separating lobby from elevators exited Merlin Jackson of the sixteenth floor, a rather old and svelte oral surgeon who could've afforded a place higher up. Without slowing or pausing, Jackson nodded his head once, as if time or decorum only allowed him to bow from the neck up, and responded, "Thanks, Oliver, you, too," and into the world he went in purple slacks and beige slip-on loafers.

Oliver returned to thoughts of himself. The pleasure of doing so aside, it was also necessary: his important project was a short film on the life of Oliver Apple. Late spring and Oliver was leaving work (as he is soon to do again). Continuing a conversation from the previous day, Regina, the woman relieving him, asked, "Have you ever played a real person?" Oliver, an unneeded track jacket hanging in his fist like polyester carrion, eyes moving upward, head tilting sideways, responded, "I don't believe so, not that I can remember." And he leaves, now wringing nonexistent water from the jacket, now draping it over his shoulder by two hooked fingers, now thinking of how exciting it would be to recreate moments of his life. A successful run as Queequeg in his early twenties, a performance one reviewer called "tremendous," preceded years of bit parts and forgettable leads—neither of which would bring critical esteem and public adoration, that double helix of eternal life—so he needed to create for himself what the world had failed to provide: a work whose sole purpose was showcasing his talents. Oliver, as recounted to every captive ear, had not been discovered (a word he detested and didn't use, because genius wasn't "discovered" but declared its own arrival) and would never be recognized without a role tailored to him. This idea, a very short biopic, was unlike anything else, and it recurred to him while on long walks, while he clipped fingernails from the undisturbed comfort of a toilet. But along the path from inspiration to realization was the disappointing discovery that his milieu of struggling actors was appallingly uncreative. They unfailingly asked, "Why not a scene from something people are familiar with?" Explained once and repeated begrudgingly thereafter: "Because I need total concentration on my performance, not whether my Creon matches the image in someone's head. The details of adaptation are irrelevant." Makes sense, they often replied. His little movie was thus far untitled but Oliver pictured a dreamy life-after-death montage shot with the help of his ex-wife (an actress) and daughter—a fusillade of enigmatic, swiftly emerging and disappearing images driven forward by a public-domain soundtrack of bougarabou drums.

Regina predictably arrived a few minutes late, but she was also less mature than her years. With collar button and tie undone, Oliver could see the forked tongue of a dragon tattoo licking the lower part of her neck. He hadn't seen the rest but envisioned a mythical scene of terrified villagers around her waist, a darkened sky across much of her upper body, the monster covering her entire right breast. In the clothed, but no less imaginary, world that right breast was separated from the left by the strap of a messenger bag, over which hung her work blazer. Regina moved with reluctance, as if every step was a prelude to running away. Resting her arms on the front desk, she leaned forward—"Hi, Oliver."—and Oliver stood and grabbed everything he needed in one motion, his blazer, a messenger bag of his own, a cup he failed to throw away earlier (protein shake).

"Hey, Regina. Long day?"

"Not really, I'm just tired."

She was always tired. "Oh, sorry to hear that. Hopefully, nothing out of the ordinary happens and you can doze while no one's watching tonight."

"I hear that." As their paths crossed, Oliver leaving what they nicknamed the command center and Regina going to it, she added, "I hope you didn't leave the seat hot like you usually do," and laughed.

"Well," he said, playing along, "Don't know if I can help that." One more counterfactual before leaving: he could send Regina to a prison camp.

<u>2</u>

A violent death was Oliver's greatest fear. Death itself was unoriginal, the body's dullest necessity, and whatever happened in the afterlife, the heavy husk perceived nothing once you were gone. But dying in pain and terror was different because you weren't dying in pain and terror but living your final moments in pain and terror—a possibility that spanned the routine horror of being tied up and tormented by burglars to recurring fantasies of wild animals, unholy claws and teeth flaying him, ripping away hands and legs before finally separating body from head. That anyone could believe he once tried to kill himself was an absurd misunderstanding: his algothanatophobia was undiagnosed but obvious. Most methods of suicide were torturous and the others, a soporific self-gassing or an expeditious gunshot to the brain, suggested emotional despair he could not understand. It was nonsense for those reasons and another, too: Oliver believed your death mattered as much as your life, and in his life, he'd yet to kiss the head of a star. For the greatest talents, of which Oliver considered himself, death was a marker on the road to posterity. Dying in his sleep or, perhaps, suddenly, rapidly from an hereditary time bomb were suitable ways to go, but he'd accomplished nothing to be remembered for. His time had not arrived. Not yet.

But Oliver's ex-wife insisted he plunged a knife into his wrist to kill himself. "What happened," as she called it whenever they still argued over its veracity, was thirteen years old by now. They had a fight that evening, triggered on the face of things by his forgetting to shut off faucets, the backdrop to which, like a domestic psych op, was the chirping fire alarm. "It's a molehill, a molehill!" he shouted, jerking the kitchen sink's handle, releasing pathetic spurts of unused water, "You do this with everything! Even with trifling shit!" Theresa, also a stage name but chosen for its melody, yelled, "You're a fucking insane person!" beat her thighs with harmless fists and left the room. That's when Oliver noticed the beeping and ransacked drawers until he found unopened 9-volt batteries, the same kind he tasted as a kid for fun. But he fumbled the packaging in his irate hands and pulled out and slammed more drawers until he found a knife. Its blade was eight inches long. Shorter ones would have worked, too. Blade down, Oliver positioned the knife's tip where cardboard met plastic, pulled back three or four inches and thrust. The immediate shock was fleeting, milliseconds of milliseconds, overtaken by pain Oliver nonsensically described as "like being shot." According to Oliver, he dropped knife and batteries and grunted, by which he meant a manly, gallant growl. But Theresa said along with the faint jangle of the knife's blade against kitchen floor she heard Oliver shriek, by which she meant a frightened, childlike cry. She contended the wound had been mostly along his wrist—not completely because he drew back from finality when he acted. Yet Oliver claimed he stabbed himself in the palm for the most part, nicking part of his wrist because of poor aim. They ignored the decisive scar.

Oliver and Theresa's relationship outlasted every prediction but their own: the educated guesses of parents and friends were that it would be rageful, exhausting, brief as cum. These opinions were uttered in the privacy of minds and bedrooms, of course, but no one hides their true face. Subtext often resides on the surface. So their skepticism was known to Oliver and Theresa, who shared an intense desire, like ill-suited lovers before them, to shut up all detractors.

Oliver recalled meeting Theresa at an acting workshop—this was after their pseudonyms, well after Oliver decided he'd be the most important actor of his generation, though about when Theresa began rethinking a similar ambition. Theresa, the amateur triathlete, Oliver remembered the pronounced sight of her collarbone running through a sleeveless, periwinkle blouse. Beltless pants, a shade of black, fitted around her waist, and the black loafers with golden buckles. Her eyes were narrow, long, stretching across a face whose tenuity was like the sign of a body that'd gotten rid of all unnecessary things. Hair fell benignly onto her shoulder blades. Almost immediately Oliver wanted to love Theresa and to be loved and burdened by her. She, likewise, considered love a hardship in which happiness was for the hereafter. And devotion to each other was how they tried to substantiate their outlooks, barreling into home buying and family life, incanting "I love you" as if they were trying to awaken a spirit. But, for them, that spirit had never walked Earth, and they eventually separated (a break would be helpful, they said), then divorced, though not because the zeal of their passion had dimmed or because they accepted being proven wrong. They divorced because they were too tired to continue. Romantic love, as Oliver and Theresa understood it, had drained their capacity to carry on as spouses. Yet, their investment allowed that ill-fated marriage to transform into a supportive, bitchy friendship. Neither desired remarriage, to each other or anyone else, but divorce had made it okay to hate—and explained their enduring attachment.

The third-floor window of Oliver's apartment looked onto the yard of his erstwhile home. During much of the year he saw just that front door, but in the right season, when trees were leafless, with complicit sunlight and sightlines, he could see through windows or spot the family car puttering along the back alley. When enough days had gone by no one noticed the weirdness: even Oliver's move from a second-floor space at a kitty-corner angle from the old house to the divine view of his current place appeared normal. But Oliver was a good boy and thought of his living arrangement as an extension of his paternal duties. He could arrive quickly if an emergency happened and his closeness had made visiting their daughter easier. That Oliver knew when a man visited Theresa wasn't a problem. Neither was knowing if they'd left that evening. Nor if his old bedroom light had gone out and they left the following morning. He considered himself protective rather than overbearing or jealous. Yet, when a man stayed over, at times he wondered if she … well, he wondered. Nobody controls what arrives in their head. Oliver looked out and down, as casually as someone uninterested in what he saw, and from the living room, his daughter Greta (as in Garbo) looked out and up. Such coincidences happened on occasion, but everyone had learned to ignore their internal whispers about who was eying whom. "They're all in," he muttered. Recalling that long-ago day, he looked at his right hand, picturing a knife in it, and lifted the left enough to see his fingers wiggle. He carried nine bottles of fake blood and unopened light bulbs in a brown paper bag, a ten-inch knife, the largest he owned, unhidden in his other hand. Oliver didn't happen upon any neighbors leaving his building, but crossing the street he waved, gripping the knife between thumb and pointer while flexing the other fingers. Greta, who was sitting in the bay window, responded first with a bemused, slow-moving wave at the sight of her approaching father, smiling and wielding a knife, then ran away, "Mom! Dad's carrying a knife and waving it around in the air!" she shouted. Oliver had a key, but that was for emergencies. He rang the bell instead.

Theresa, opening the door, snapped, "What's wrong with you? Get in here before someone calls the police."

"What's wrong with me?" His forehead itched near the widow's peak. He scratched with a thumbnail, knife angled hornlike above his head. "This?" pointing with his eyes, "I was coming right over. Not like I was making stops in between. You overreact all the time."

"You're walking around with a knife and waving it above your head in broad daylight and I'm overreacting?"

"Yes. You are. And I wasn't waving it around. I saw Greta in the window and waved. I can't wave to my daughter?"

"You can wave all you want, but not with some massive knife in your hand. And why did you bring that anyway? You were afraid we didn't have knives?"

Greta cut in, "Dad, that was dumb. What if somebody thought you were a crazy person?"

Oliver replied to Greta, "No one would think that," and to his ex-wife, "I brought the knife because I wanted to make sure we had one that was big enough. Regardless, I can't do this with you. Not today. Any other day but today. You know how important this is to me: why start in now?"

Theresa rocked her head, rolled her eyes, "I'm not starting anything with you. Sorry if you think my being worried is an imposition."

"Being worried is fine. Being histrionic, and on a day like today, is different." Oliver walked toward the kitchen, Theresa and Greta following, "I spent all day practically, just trying to find that place again, and I come in and poof! you're sniping at me. I mean, goddamn, can you cut me a little slack when we're about to start this thing?"

"I'm not sniping. You talk about me, but you take everything to ten," Theresa said, raising her hand above her head, "It's DEF-CON 1 with you all the time."

"DEFCON 5 is the worst."

"No, it's 1."

"You should know."

"Dad," Greta interrupted, "I just think she was worried something would happen to you. I was, too. But we're here to help."

Oliver put the knife and bag on the counter, ran a hand through Greta's hair then placed her head on his chest.

Working backwards, Oliver figured Greta must have been a piddly zygote when "what happened" happened, but her presence at its recreation lifted atoms of regret into the air. She resembled her mother and maternal grandmother and maternal great-grand-mother. Her eyes were narrow and wide, and like those women had done at her age, Greta's hair was long and plaited and draped over her left shoulder. Nevertheless, Oliver believed she was more like him—in the way they saw the world, how she would, if the opportunity arose, bend towards the light of her own sun as he was doing. Greta went for a tripod, moving past Theresa, who reached out and rubbed her back as she passed, and without remorse, Oliver would have exchanged them for the life he'd envisioned since childhood, a life in which Greta's existence or even remembering Theresa were impossible. He could not fantasize about a world of stardom and permanence without regretting the one he inhabited and the man was honest enough to follow disappointment to its logical conclusion. Greta returned, smiled at him: "Where should I set it up, Daddy?" she asked.

Oliver's based-on-true-events version of this episode was without a chirping fire alarm. Instead, he'd stab himself trying to open the package of light bulbs. They had no script, just a loose outline of what was to transpire: Theresa, in fact, had no idea how Oliver would maim himself and figured the light bulbs had been carried along mistakenly or brought as an overly solicitous gift. Before they began, she told him, "Don't accidentally do it for real." Oliver replied, "I know what I'm doing." Whether the phone was stationed in the tripod or held in her hands, Greta was instructed to get as little of Theresa's face in the frame as possible—and preferably none. She'd be a voice, a pate, a back, a set of flailing hands, a presence co-fueling his rendezvous with misadventure. An unhealthy dose of will power kept Greta composed through a few takes—reenactment of the upstairs raucous, their initial shouting and name-calling, the final, ominous tromping downstairs—but she conceded to grief when they first shot the stabbing scene. Oliver, grimacing, his face transformed into a thousand demented angles like a broken windowpane, jerking the faucet handle and screaming, "You bitch! Every time you do this to me! You petty, crazy fucking bitch! I hate you! Out! Out! Out! Out! Now! Get out now, you cunt!" Theresa, who admittedly hadn't expected that degree of bitterness or that she'd feel glutted with unreleased bile, responded likewise, "You're a fucking psychopath! Don't break my goddamn handle!"

"It's mine, too!" he snarled, "I'll do whatever the fuck I want!"

"Why did I marry you! I hate your fucking guts! You're loony, you should be locked away! If you don't have a fucking stroke first!"

"Get out!"

"You know what: I hope you do have a stroke, I hope you die, you deserve it you worthless piece of shit!"

Greta wept, behind shut eyes and fastened lips and hands covering both, unseen by her parents. Oliver started rifling through kitchen drawers. "What are you doing now!" Theresa yelled, "Now you wanna break everything in the house!"

"A light bulb! That's why I committed the crime of leaving the faucet on upstairs: I realized it's just too goddamn dark everywhere! Our bedroom is like a whorehouse: is that the look you want!"

Theresa stomped away, legitimately upset with the past and the present, and Oliver grabbed a knife, his knife, along with the package of light bulbs. Greta had opened her eyes and witnessed Oliver pretending to stab himself. He screamed louder, with more agony than he had in reality. Greta screamed, too, and nearly fainted. It took close to an hour to calm her down. "It was too real," she repeated, which Oliver also understood to mean, "Your acting was tremendous." (Theresa, too, who'd given up acting proper and become a one-woman consulting shop, using the lessons of acting to teach mid-level managers how to think quickly and thoughtfully on their feet, beamed inside at her performance.) They continued after Greta was better collected. Among other images, they needed to get shots of Oliver stumbling then falling, scowling and writhing and hallucinating on the kitchen floor, wetted by a lakelet of fake blood. Greta appeared unruffled thereafter.

<u>3</u>

The futuristic twenty-first century had reached young adulthood, but cloning his twelve-year-old self or time traveling to impregnate Theresa about a decade ago remained impossible. A son would have been lovely given what he needed—an uncommon thought for Oliver. Sons, for a man, were threats to individuality, though a little guy who shared his face offered a solution to his cinematic problem. Such dilemmas require radical answers, however, and science was no help with an existential crisis. Oliver was handcuffed by facts, so he did what humanity had always done: compromised between desire and reality.

The summer of his thirteenth birthday, the hoped-for year of puberty in full bloom, Oliver took a four-hour train ride alone. He was visiting family at their country home and his first solo trip reinforced the sense of himself as a man in-progress. Nervous but ordering himself to appear calm, Oliver clenched the handle of a small duffle bag and his tumid backpack forced him to lean forward as he walked the platform. At his car's entrance, the conductor, a rather large person who stood with her hips forward and chin back, scribbled "06," his seat assignment, on a rectangular slip of paper. Oliver turned, waved to the family he was leaving for a couple of weeks then boarded. That he suddenly arrived at the frontier of crying was a mistake. Oliver squeezed his eyes and shook his head and made it go away. His backpack initially wouldn't fit into the overhead compartment, regardless the angle he tried, and unable to endure more anxiety and irritation, Oliver shoved and punched it, stood on his seat and delivered forearm shivers to the groaning luggage. When that was over, he noticed a handful of passengers eying him, to which he responded with a shamefaced grin and placed the duffel bag at his feet. Next to Oliver in the window seat he coveted was an older man whose fingers and breath were stained with the cheddar-and-caramel popcorn he was eating (a knockoff of the name-brand stuff). The train moved. Oliver laid his head back, eyes shifting between scenery and passengers. A pair of legs, three rows in front of him, extended into the aisle and withdrew. She looked back—a thin face and narrow eyes, brown hair dyed with a streak of grey—and reclined, stretched her legs, and withdrew them again. Oliver fidgeted, anticipating a physiological response that had yet to occur, and the young woman stood, reached into the overhead compartment. She wore a professional team's basketball shorts of faded black, a blue-and-white striped golf shirt, running sneakers, and rummaged a neck pillow out of her things. She sat, for good, and her legs again came out. Because going to the restroom was no longer safe, Oliver put the duffle bag on his lap, head rested on his aisle-side hand, expecting he'd settle into a pleasing trip of semi-arousal.

Oliver had begun to doze. His thoughts were submerged beneath the surface of consciousness when the train made its one stop between his departure and destination. He awoke, lap safely covered, with a nondescript hard-on, pre-ejaculate having dripped and dribbled into his underwear during the ride's first hour. His clouded eyes grasped the woman's legs, then touched the face of another woman standing above him. "Is this my stop?" he wondered. Signage outside said it was not.

"Excuse me, I believe this is my seat." The woman had a duffle bag, too, slung over her shoulder, and next to her a carry-on suitcase, its handle extended. Her short hair appeared to be attached to the baseball cap she wore, as if it were part of a Halloween costume, and she showed Oliver a rectangular slip of paper on which was written "6."

Oliver, careful not to let his cover fall, angled his bottom toward the older man, reached into a back pocket. "I don't think so … " he timidly replied, showing his seat assignment. "Unless they gave us the same one?"

The woman took his paper, held it next to hers: "I don't think so. I believe this is my seat." She looked around, "Excuse me," she called to the conductor, "Excuse me, I believe this is my seat."

Oliver scanned the car. A few eyes and foreheads had risen

over their seats, the young woman had turned partway to face him, legs crossed in the aisle, and the conductor had still not arrived. She moved laboriously, gripping headrests for balance though the train had yet to move. The woman was a little overheated: "I believe this is my seat. This is my seat. I believe he's sitting in my seat."

"It's my seat," Oliver said, meeker than he knew, and the other passenger shook her head as if doing so would erase his response.

Pressing the seat assignments into the conductor's face: "This is my seat isn't it? I'm six and this is six."

Slips of paper in hand, eyeing the numerals longer than seemed reasonable, "Sir, you're seat ninety," and she flashed the number to Oliver and turned it right-side up, "You have to move," and Oliver thought, "She called me 'sir,'" with pride.

Ah—Bu—Ah ... , Oliver emitted a series of half-sounds before saying, "But where's seat ninety? Since I'm here, can we just switch?"

"No, this is my seat," the woman answered.

The conductor, who didn't care where either of them sat, gave a look of fatigue, acquiesced, "It's up that way," pointing towards the car's front.

With delay Oliver hoped to better his position, but deferral and commotion didn't force the tiny edifice to collapse: it was if onlookers had made him harder. Oliver inexplicably turned to his seatmate, who, having just eaten a mound of popcorn from the hollow of his hand, pecked and licked his raised, stretched out palm and responded with eyes of indifference.

"Sir, please," the conductor said.

Oliver couldn't tell if the passenger were about to cry or scream at him: her eyes reddened and the lips were turned down, her chest rose and fell at an easy, agitated rhythm. Keeping the duffle bag tucked at his crotch, Oliver leaped from his seat, shoved by the conductor and passenger, and ran down the aisle baying as the train started to move. He, at first, passed seat 90, paused quietly, began howling again, and finding his seat, sat and remained there in silence until his stop.

This isn't the story he told Theresa and Greta: to their deaths, his daughter and ex-wife would believe he'd been forced out of his seat due to the conductor's sloppy penmanship and that person along with a passenger bullying him. Oliver's ursine response was an expression of righteous anger, of justifiable self-defense. They, consequently, recorded Oliver stumbling through the aisle of a partially empty train, jostling riders while grunting under breath with a semi-frenetic expression. Although one gentleman cocked forearm crosswise to his chest preparing an undelivered backhand blow, no one responded violently. Oliver indulged his convulsions of rage, screaming and, at times, beating his chest—he'd been in some fights as a kid and in a four-against-two brawl as a teenager (on the majority's side)—but fisticuffs were ultimately something other people did. He was a yeller not a fighter and wisely chose which passengers to elbow past. Having moved between four railcars, he was confronted entering his fifth. The conductor wore a uniform of navy blue pants, jacket, and V-neck sweater to which he added a white-and-red-striped tie: a five o'clock shadow was crowding out what had been a thin, finely trimmed mustache. An otherwise unnoticeable man of average height and obvious but unworrying girth, the glint of his nametag and lapel pin—the company logo, swooshes of wind spelling Xpress—and buttons at his torso and cuffs, the brass of his clothed-topped hat gave him the look of an amateur colonel. He stopped Oliver. Theresa, who was holding the camera, stopped behind him. Greta, who'd been following Theresa, walked into her mother.

"What are you doing? You can't be running through here," his eyes tennis-watching Oliver and Theresa, "You don't have a permit for this."

"We need a permit?" Oliver responded, "I thought you could record whatever you wanted. It's just a phone."

"Yeah, if you're just recording, but it looks like you're shooting a movie or something. You can't do *that* without a permit." He'd emphasized "that" as if the word might be lost in translation or misinterpreted as referring to something else—walking, for instance, or standing in the aisles, perhaps boarding the train altogether.

"I didn't know that—"

"Right."

"We'll go back to our seats."

Oliver turned to leave but the conductor said, "No. You're getting off at the next stop."

After ushering a handful of new passengers aboard, the conductor signaled all clear and mounted the train's steps. His soles had begun to wear and his arms, using rails to each side, did as much to lift him into the train as his tiring legs. Then he looked back and shook his head while removing his sweaty hat. In one direction the platform extended into sets of illuminated stairs leading upward to the station, and from the other, a fall wind entered and train tracks straightened into a sunless horizon. Oliver, Theresa, and Greta weren't lost but someplace between where they started and where they hadn't planned to arrive.

<u>4</u>

Theresa never had a traditional wedding dress: they were married at a downtown courthouse by a judge, an older woman with white hair and brown eyes who presided over their everlasting promise like a supportive but displeased aunt. She also no longer had the clothes she wore that morning. Oliver, though, wanted to relive that moment, loosely and in the same clothes but without capturing Theresa's face.

Since her adolescence Theresa wanted a summer wedding and waterfront reception, about this she was romantic, and remembered wearing a long, white billowing skirt with streaks of cardinal print. The sleeves of her white t-shirt covered just her shoulders and its neckline fell into a U. Those old, tan sandals were eventually tossed out because the loops around her big toes had come apart. Oliver remembered Theresa in denim overall shorts with cuffed hems, a red-and-black flannel shirt unbuttoned at the neck and rolled up at the sleeves. They agreed on her shoes, but Theresa was more correct about what she wore than Oliver. Her shirt was sleeveless and the skirt's print a salmon shade of pink, whereas the outfit Oliver recalled was from the day after when they celebrated with friends at the beach. The groom's clothing was easier to re-picture. Oliver's main concern then, hurried nuptials aside, had been his role as a police detective. His part in the whole thing was minor, yet this was also Oliver's period of "staying in character." He, therefore, married Theresa dressed as Detective Calbert Hampton. His out-of-place attire was a deep blue suit and polished black dress shoes, which he purchased to upgrade his stage clothes, aviators he owned and used in the production, and a small notebook protruding from a breast pocket, an accent the director had disallowed. Oliver cleverly interpreted Detective Hampton as reserved, difficult to read, unforgiving of sarcasm, and a teddy bear beneath the skin of his passé masculinity. Being "in character" meant taciturnity and periodic smiles, and none of it was necessary for the role: Detective Hampton had a couple dozen lines mostly in the second scene of the play's first act. A person of his artistic self-regard would deny it, but Oliver, in deed, believed every entrepreneurial cliché. His modus operandi, had he been aware of the quote (or thought it was uttered by von Goethe), was in effect, "Everything comes to him who hustles while he waits." Theresa worrying (to herself) he wouldn't break character for their I-dos was justified—Oliver (to himself) had considered staying in character—yet when the time arrived, he swore immortal love before God and State as Oliver Apple.

Oliver motioned to the ground, as if showing where the rebels had fallen: "We're going to stand here, Greta, not too far out. Just enough to get our upper bodies. Then we'll move back and do more to get our legs in the shot, which will be a little difficult, I know, because I'm taller. Then we'll do some full-body shots from behind. With those we'll also do a few walking away. Head to toe. Or head to heel, I suppose." He grasped her hand, winked.

Their setting, a cul-de-sac blocks from where they lived: the road paused at a small, cordoned-off sylvan area overlooking a riverbank; tangerine and cocoa-brown leaves dampened by the morning rain covered the pavement, stuck to the surface of cars around them. Oliver held Theresa's hand, let go and locked arms instead. Deep breaths were taken. Oliver swallowed first and Theresa soon afterwards and the sounds of their own saliva resonated in their ears, forced them to wonder if what they did had been audible to the other. "It's acting," they repeated in the solitude of their heads. Theresa wore a grey herringbone coat, buttoned up, the free hand kept warm in a pocket, while Oliver by happenstance wore a black peacoat buttoned up with a hand pocketed as well. He hadn't expected speaking as little as he did, but he and Theresa adjusted their positions with almost no words spoken. The most frequent sound was Greta's sniffles, which she wiped away with tissues before running out and using the sleeve of her grey herringbone coat, like her mother's. By the time that day's work was nearly done, her sleeves were being used to wipe away tears. Shoulders heaving as if her torso were trying to rip itself from her lower half, she turned away and wouldn't be consoled. When Theresa or Oliver tried to place an arm around her, Greta slapped back their hands and took a few steps. Finally, however, she turned to her parents, and crying into her hands, whimpered, "We used to be a family." Oliver and Theresa took her into a brief, ill-fitting hug. The parents' hands, careful a finger or palm didn't rest too long on the other's arm or back, patted around as if a room they knew well had darkened. But notwithstanding some modest words of comfort, little was said.

"Oh, Gret, it'll be okay, we're a family," Theresa told her. She looked at Oliver, who responded with a softened voice, "Yeah."

"We don't have to live in one house to be a family. Dad's right across the street and we love you. That's all that matters." She again looked at Oliver.

"We don't have to live together. We love you." Eyeing Theresa, now rubbing her back with husbandly confidence, "And we love each other, too. That'll never change."

Greta needed to be reassured, but her misery was inspiring. He waited, holding the back of her arm and stroking with a thumb as if to say, "Feel your feelings … but not forever," though whether she was nearing the end he couldn't tell. After rummaging unsuccessfully in his coat pockets for a loose tissue or scrap of paper Greta could wipe her nose with, Oliver suggested they all be in the last shot: arm in arm, walking away from the camera. Considering the final memory he planned to record, it surprised him that involving Greta hadn't come about, but the idea touched him like the warmth of putting on socks freshly removed from the dryer. Daughter standing between them, Oliver and Theresa and Greta formed a triptych of dysfunction, but for the instant, resembled bliss.

<u>5</u>

Greta was a healthy newborn of about eight-and-a-half pounds and a smidge less than eighteen inches long. Oliver believed she was the cutest baby he'd seen and loved her more than he knew possible, but he was also revulsed at having created a doughy, helpless human-creature and about what it meant for his freedom. He was a provider now, someone who'd made himself second in his world, which staring adoringly at his baby girl, seemed unnatural. Watching her squirm, her erratic fists, that arms and legs so small and delicate could function was mystifying. He wanted to embrace Greta forever—at the risk of smothering her to death. Theresa had looked weary and pale and shared his ambivalence, though neither suspected it of their spouse. They kept love in their eyes and disquiet in their hearts. She was also having the type of second thoughts that arise after getting what you want: in her case, a natural birth. Mom's labor and daughter's first breath had occurred in a hospital room, a fact so common one needn't describe the doctor's habit of snapping her fingers when she talked, but insofar as everything he envisioned, Oliver daydreamed of constructing a mock maternity ward and filling it with actors in variegated medical scrubs. But this idea occurred before money and time burst through the locked door of his imagination, and like before, pecuniary, workaday, unartistic concerns forced him to reinvent the truth.

Ergo, Theresa was lying in bed, propped up by the elbows, a blanket draped over her bent, spread-open knees, having gone into labor unexpectedly—screaming profanities at the world, insults at Oliver, unloosing shrieks neighbors could hear. Despite a mother's role in childbirth, Oliver would not be overshadowed. A phone clamped between his ear and shoulder, he ducked in and out of the blanket, punctuating his close-ups with demands that Theresa, to give one example, "Shut the fuck up and listen!" He especially liked his way of pointing at her. Each time Oliver aimed his finger, he could see its tip sharpening into a blade and lengthening until pricking her breastbone, never drawing blood, just pressing enough to make her feel what it'd be like if it had: again what he pictured could not be reproduced. With the retelling of her birth, however, Greta was having fun. The conceit of Theresa birthing at home, their screaming during the fake labor, that Oliver would effectively handle a delivery, rubbed against Greta's reality so violently that she smiled and giggled and laughed and blushed with the embarrassment Theresa and Oliver lacked. Her response caused them to cast about for more ways to denigrate: they predictably needed to be angrier, more realistic. At some (nonsensical) point, Oliver screamed, "I don't even know if it's mine!" and later, after saying he'd take "his baby" away from her, Theresa responded, "I'll kill her and me before you take my child!" Nothing. Greta laughed. Her parents seethed.

Outside four police officers charged from their vehicles and circled the house. More were stationed behind open cruiser doors with guns drawn and lights flashing. Greta abandoned the scene of her mom and dad and looked out: she was the first to hear sirens, the muffled announcement over a bullhorn. Her parents stopped shouting. They could hear a helicopter circling overhead as Greta ran from the window: "A bunch of policemen are outside and running around the house!" She was crying again.

Oliver moved closer, guardedly, as if his footfalls could be heard outside, and peeled an edge of the curtain back with an index and middle finger.

"Get away from that window, Oliver!" Theresa yelled.

"Shhh, it's fine."

Through a sliver between curtain and window frame, Oliver counted at least a dozen officers wielding handguns and rifles. An armored vehicle was nearby, too. Onlookers had gathered in the windows of his apartment building, and farther away, outside his field of vision, busybodies stood at a row of police barricades alongside a local TV news crew. He yanked the curtains open. Theresa, who'd pressed herself into a wall with Greta cocooned in her arms, yelled again, "Oliver, get away from that window! What are you doing!" So much background noise … The bedroom, Oliver's old bedroom, had casement windows that he pushed open as he had some bygone winter mornings to wake Theresa with cold air. His motions were exaggerated, he moved as if in a comic ballet. "Oliver!" Theresa covered her face and shielded Greta's eyes, the girl pleaded, "Daddy!" Oliver Apple leaned out and spread his arms, as if to embrace the leaden, fiery, purblind wasps that could swarm and pierce everything he knew, and proclaimed:

> Tomorrow, and tomorrow, and tomorrow,
> Creeps in this petty pace from day to day,
> To the last syllable of recorded time;
> And all our yesterdays have lighted fools
> The way to dusty death. Out, out, brief candle!

Life's but a walking shadow, a poor player,
That struts and frets his hour upon the stage,
And then is heard no more. It is a tale
Told by an idiot, full of sound and fury,
Signifying nothing.

Part II

1

No one would expect a persecuted man to look as good as I do, would expect the face that made me famous and powerful still vibrant—and as a woman no less. The betrayals I'm enduring, the shabby dress I'm wearing don't matter. My lips are full, colored an amorous red, alluring as a starlet's. But self-discoveries are always surprises. Knowledge of oneself, if you follow, is a little exercise in discovering how protean you are. Each of us is a performer and leading a nation is not very different from enchanting an audience. Had chance, amoral and indifferent chance, unfolded another way, I would've been remembered alongside Denzel and Gassman. Instead, whether I survive or not, I shall certainly be defamed another Salazar or Somoza. But, in life, we encounter twists and turns and twists and turns again.

The Republic of Ayapaya is closer to the United States than Los Angeles is to New York City, but flying directly from the US is impossible. This unfortunate state of affairs isn't a matter of terrain, but a consequence of history. A fact I was unaware of until my trip to the country. Yet, my travels didn't begin at a North American airport. Millenia ago peoples emerged across the globe that would someday place me here … but solving that archaeological riddle is the work of historians. I date my role to a nearer past. I was completely inexperienced with film editing and unshakably opposed to hiring an editor. For the same reasons you wouldn't hand your child and car keys to a stranger with directions to see them home safely. Some tasks cannot be trusted to anyone. Besides, with a kidnapped child one can call the police, but no jurisdiction issues Amber Alerts for missing dreams. Which is why the risk of failing at my own hands was preferable to the chance of succeeding at another's. The events of my last five or six months notwithstanding, I remain an American of the United States type. But film editing was more difficult than anticipated. Between imagination and realization lay an unpaved road, which caused a weekend to drift into a week into a couple months of sustained, solitary labor. But unlike other, less self-sufficient humans, my whole life I'd maintained a social circlet. Most people were kept just beyond the outstretched fingertips of arm's length. I was prepared, as all artists must be, for creative isolation. Although, I confess, my isolation was relative. I needed to earn a living and visits to Greta and Theresa continued but were much less frequent. Had Theresa or Greta thought I was deserting them, I couldn't have dedicated myself as fervently as I did to my project. Good fathers don't abandon their daughters or their exes. Unless they're no alternatives. But thankfully, mother and daughter were stoic, they carried on as if my presence were immaterial, and monitoring the house from my apartment still took little exertion. Nothing before had required as much effort as finishing this film. Acting is my first and last creative love, but it issues from me naturally. Every second of preparation and study was corralling and directing an element which otherwise would have surged uncontrollably. For the uncommonly gifted, studying one's craft is turning nuclear fission into nuclear power. But making even a very, very short movie demanded something else of me and that something else required time. My daughter and former wife gave all the freedom and support I needed. Regina, conversely, was a nuisance. After a couple of weeks had passed, fourteen days in which I spent eighty fruitless hours at my job, I began taking my old laptop to work. That computer was a bowl game of poorly labeled files that hindered progress. Haphazard underscores, malicious numerals at the caboose of generic filenames. I'd built for myself a labyrinth of evocative mirages. Hours must have been spent opening files I believed were others, and I admit better organization would have been helpful, but in a more rational world doing so would be the job of someone else. A person like Theresa, for instance. She knew me better than anyone and could interpret, with my forceful oversight, what I envisioned, as mothers decipher the cries of their infants. But she knew as little about editing as me, and by the end of filming, it was obvious she'd given all she was going to give me. Until then I'd never experienced greater stress. I required absolute sacrifice of myself and those around me. I could not suffer a person who didn't understand artistic creation, the excitement of chasing a star across your internal sky. I sound romantic because I am. This might be an unpopular opinion. Not democratic enough for our era, but I don't apologize for believing in art. Regina did not believe in art. She read whatever books and poems had been assigned in high school. She'd seen plenty of movies and plays, but she did not believe in art. What Regina believed in was entertainment. For people like her, every iamb of art was a product one gobbled up passing from watery womb to gelid grave. So, for me, our discussions about my short lingered much longer than their brevity. Given the setup of monitors at our security desk, my laptop was perfectly inconspicuous. At most a handful of residents noticed, and of those who did, none cared about what transpired on-screen. I just needed to keep the volume low, look up and smile while addressing whomever with a few anodyne sentences, and I was free to continue. I did, initially, ensure my things were put away before Regina's arrival, but fear of being caught and ratted out lessened. I concluded, without knowing I'd concluded, Regina wasn't a threat, so I could work until she appeared for her shift. Four or five days into this arrangement and she finally commented: "What are you doing back there? I see you with that computer every day now." Her frisky, unsuspicious tone was a poor mask for nosiness. I told her, "A short—a short movie—a little project I have in the works."

"A movie?" she responded. Regina's eyes widened as if I were sharing with her titillating office gossip. "I didn't know you made movies. What kind of movie?"

By "kind of movie" I'm definite she meant "plot." I would never yell at a coworker unless it were necessary, but I was becoming angry. Not irrepressibly, though enough to realize I had to control myself. I answered, "It's about my life, important moments, things like that."

"Are you in it?" she blurted, smiling and eyeballing me as if I were remade by her new knowledge. I performed enthusiasm: "Of course, it's my life! Who else would be in it? You think I have Denzel's number!" She playfully slapped my shoulder with the back of her hand as we crossed paths: "Make sure I see it when you're done." I smiled and smiled but didn't respond. Thereafter, she wanted updates when I saw her and pried for more details. Regina, this was most aggravating, also suggested memories she believed were humorous. Placing art in hands like hers is as foolish as leaving war to generals. I declined Regina's ideas, but even so, her suggestions sneaked into my head on occasion and more time was squandered remembering what another person believed was important. Because of her, I thought of Samuel Brown, Esq., formerly of the nineteenth floor, a middle-aged man less successful than his father. Regardless of season or time of day, he checked the mail and held court in his wan, pinkish bare feet. His gait was like a thousand small water splashes against the floor, swift but unrushed. I also recalled Herman Miller and Olivia Mills-Miller, commercial brokers and residents of the nineteenth floor as well. Propping the front doors open with their feet and elbows, they dropped bags of groceries one afternoon and scurrying free with fruits and vegetables was a humble, beige dildo. They hurried to it, but Mills-Miller arrived first and snatched it up as if their confidant had been lodged in the Mica flooring. To be frank, the toy was admirably realistic, and seeing it clutched in her otherwise benign hand and tossed in a paper bag made me wince and shield my lap. Worse than her ill-influence, Regina's interest was also superficial. Some of the world's most capable officials assured me with near total certainty that she watched my short just once; forwarded the link to a cousin; and closed her browser. Moreover, with the face of a former coworker internationally known, the difficulties in Ayapaya unmissable to any sentient adult with internet, she accessed not one article, newsclip, or podcast about the drama taking place in her hemisphere. That Regina believed "It was really interesting," as she told me between shifts, means nothing. She's lucky: my vengeance is discerning. Regardless, art like *A Brief Life* does not think of her as its audience. The title occurred to me looking from my apartment window. My eyes ambled up and down the street, before pausing where Greta and Theresa lived, the home that had also been mine. Although I was yawning at dusk, I thought back to the afternoon when policemen surrounded the house. Of what I saw that day, the most absurd was a chopper floating joylessly below the clouds, an image that delighted me until the day I could no longer dilly-dally with simple pleasures. I pushed the window open and flicked my wrists as if scattering a mind-controlling dust into the wind. When my face met the cool, tart autumn air, I saw police aiming guns at me. Not a barrel was pointed elsewhere. As the state decided when it dropped all charges, disorderly conduct and whatnot, my actions were spontaneous, perhaps foolish, but ultimately harmless. I started speaking—not fearlessly, because I didn't feel anything. I noticed, of course, faces pressed against windows across the street, and in particular, a baby-faced police officer who'd been rushing toward the house before crouching onto a knee when I entered the scene. I was old enough to be his extremely young father. An announcement followed my last words: "Show us your hands, don't move!" I showed them my hands, held my hands wide and aloft as if I had more to say, but these were speechless gestures. Perhaps a number of the policemen wondered if I was the perpetrator or a victim. Theresa has a distinct scream. I've heard it in anger, in happiness, in fear and surprise, there's an operatic warble at its highest volume, so I knew the scream I heard was Greta's. Afraid for my daughter, I ducked back inside. Theresa covered Greta's mouth, and when it was over, our daughters' front teeth were stained with a little of her mother's blood. The rest happened quickly. Beneath us doors and windows were smashed open, shouts from masked men in fatigues pointing carbines, and I was dragged downstairs with my legs and hands shackled. Remembrances of what happened, of sitting chained on the living room floor watching teary Greta and downcast Theresa explain what happened, I thought, "A brief life." Forgiveness was not immediate from either of them. But Greta resisted longer than her mother and I feared she was lost to me forever. At that time, I couldn't access her inmost thoughts. To glean her feelings I listened to her, observed how she behaved, and hoped Theresa clued me in to whatever else I needed to know. Yet, these are inefficient tools, most obviously because we hide in our skin. Intolerable as it is to accept, we are disguised to everyone. But, months later, with more sophisticated, electronic means, I was reassured discovering how she struggled emotionally and wanted to reconnect during the frigid months between my arrest and my leaving the United States. It also pleases me that privately, away from reporters who pester them, she now speaks and writes of me with undeniable tenderness and fears I will be killed in this nauseating country. Hugging my daughter again will mean this farcical episode is in our past. Being older, more aware that in life hellish things happen, Theresa relented before Greta. Pages of emails and texts verify my hunch she remained angry, but she was also mature enough to know nothing in our triad would change. Blood is forever and law cannot undo the love it ratified. Though embittered, Theresa allowed me to host the premiere of *A Brief Life* at their house. Gloomy Greta stayed in her bedroom, but this absence aroused in me images and sensations of the day after Theresa and I married. Other than Maroon and Ron, theatre friends of ours, each person who came to the wedding party attended my showing. The wedding I struggle to recall. Theresa was underdressed in denim overall shorts and with some embarrassment stood next to me in my prim, elegant blue suit. Officiating the ceremony was an overexcited judge who kept wishing us well. But grasping the following day causes me to remember a lyric from the American Standards my parents listened to, "The song that plays forever, my love, is the song that plays in my heart." We lazed on a patchwork of different-sized, many-colored blankets and towels. The lake's mist was warm, soothing, and wavelets tiptoed ashore, curious about our gathering. Theresa wore a sleeveless shirt and a beautiful skirt with streaks of pink that fluttered in the wind. And if she sat quickly, it rose and floated to the ground, settling over her bended legs from pale arches to narrow hips. Unwittingly, we had only invited couples. Dwayne and Whitley arrived first. He sported a pair of medicinal sunglasses with circular frames and Whitley moved with a light, aristocratic air. As happened years later for my premiere, John Dorian's wife couldn't make it and he came with his best friend, Christopher. Somehow they carried towels, food, and beer with Christopher semi-spooning on John Dorian's blue scooter. Helmeted, walking towards us, they were like misshapen astronauts. An overlong meeting at work had delayed Pamela and James, but crowded beach notwithstanding, I recognized them at a distance before they noticed us. His tall, gangly, unimposing frame, her slightly hunched yet cheerful posture. The eight of us talked and laughed, ate and drank more than our limits. We stayed at the shore through nightfall and into almost total darkness. Our illumination was starlight, crystalline in sky and water, and a smattering of illicit bonfires briefly marking the sands. As unforgettable evenings invariably do, we parted with the promise of meeting again soon, but that night and our reunion were separated by years. I started by thanking them for coming, glibly adding that Ron and Maroon's presence had made the sequel better than the original. They applauded when the lights were silenced, someone whistled. I surreptitiously watched their faces in the television's glow, but eyes that squinted, eyes that blinked, teeth that bit into lips were useless signs of thoughts and feelings. When it was over, they applauded once more and the lights returned. I remember a spectrum of indecipherable smiles, Theresa standing with arms folded then nibbling on the tip of a thumb. Maroon said, "Oliver, I really like it. I know someone else who made a short film on their phone, but it didn't come out nearly as well." All were effusive and appeared sincere, Theresa especially. She also saw *A Brief Life* the first time that evening but withheld her opinion until everyone had spoken. Seemingly liberated, she then praised what *we* had done. I believed her and the compliments that preceded them as much as my skepticism allowed. From green-eyed Mrs. Morell through my Ayapayan advisers, I doubted the words and intentions of other people with few exceptions. This people-to-people business is untrustworthy. Likewise, the one thing I'll miss when I'm back in the States is the ability to know what someone tells themself. Because of that, I know their kudos that evening were genuine. James and Pamela shared an inside joke that my "rage" reminded them of a volatile coworker, but all else they said privately was admiring. And Theresa, steadfast Theresa, was truly impressed.

By the time it was scrubbed from the internet, *A Brief Life* had just eighty-three views. And though I never cared to know who most of these people were, I was curious about the commenters. Their words and usernames made them less abstract. I imagined a theatre audience of blurred faces and my coming to Ayapaya gave them life. A representative comment was left by Cabbage_man87, who wrote, "Yo wtf did I just watch. lol." This person I pictured in their twenties, single, and without a steady job, but he was, in real life, a thirty-something-year-old man with an entrepreneurial streak. Donald Cabbage was born in 1987 and belonged to that class of optimist whose next idea is always better than their last. Another I recall is the emojis left by Lillypadthai, 😟😫🤢🧍🙆🤪, i.e., Lillian Thompson, a twenty-three-year-old with a Thai father and American mother. Color me surprised an Education degree produces a teacher with this level of insight. But I was mistaken during the early days of my rule to focus as much energy as I did on the Cabbages and Lillians of my American life. I ordered the phones and computers of theirs and others be destroyed with a little malicious code while truer enemies were nearer to me. In my American days, the only feedback that mattered was delivered by someone whose real name is unknown. I was later assured it was Ramón, but he introduced himself to me not sixty seconds from the front doors after work as Leopold. Across the street to my right was a small playground. I recall a man kneeled, cooing into a stroller while another kid competed for attention, propelling himself higher and higher in a swing. To my left, more buildings, condominiums and balconies, except for the alley, where I looked in passing. This is when I habitually unearthed the phone from my pocket, checked the time for the second time in five minutes and ignored newsletters I'd signed up for. But that day my phone flashed with an incoming call. No number, it said, "Private." I answered and "Hello, Oliver Apple?" he asked. "That's me," I told him, "Who are you?" Leopold/Ramón said he was an Ayapayan movie producer, that I fitted perfectly a role for which he was casting. It was a leading part, playing the ruler of that small Central American country. I now wonder if the Ayapayan records I saw of this encounter were authentic or sham documents provided by traitors. From the beginning, a clique of bureaucrats and high-ranking officers undermined me, so this level of duplicity wouldn't have been too filthy for them. Be that as it may, the records confirmed we chatted as I walked about three blocks westward and my initial suspicion lessened somewhat because of flattery. I won't deny that conclusion but will add praise works best when paired with reality. That afternoon's conversation was relatively short, but we agreed to meet in person. I kept this call from Theresa and met Leopold/Ramón at a hotel restaurant close to Happy Gardens a week later. He'd reserved a table, though I guessed who he was before the hostess led me to him. Leopold/Ramón sat in the middle of the dining area, sunlight and an empty chair setting up our two shot. His mustache was a squiggly bracket over his narrow, purplish lips and a triangular patch of hair decorated his chin; he wore a mint green jacket; and extending his right hand to me, Leopold/Ramón wiped his forehead with the tip of his unused middle finger. "Oliver

Apple, nice to meet you," he said. I met his hand and replied, "Likewise. It's nice to have a face for the voice." Our meeting was supposed to be over lunch, but I wasn't hungry and neither was Leopold/Ramón. He, however, drank three black coffees with a skosh of milk in each and ate half a buttered roll. Leopold/Ramón said he loved coffee and "One should eat a little whenever taking in lots of liquids. All animals need food and drink, it's how we evolved. Separating them goes against nature." I survived with a florid tea. I told Leopold/Ramón I'd never heard of Ayapaya's leader and no pictures of the man seemed to exist, not Wikipedia nor *The World Factbook* were particularly insightful; he countered Ayapaya was an introspective nation but the president had ruled a decade and his people loved him more than they loved themselves. When I called Ayapaya "reclusive," Leopold/Ramón wagged his finger, tut-tutting as he sipped coffee. Finishing, he wiped his lips with the palm of his hand and answered, "We don't meddle in the affairs of others. We believe people should live as they like as we want to live as we like—free of interference." His face never lost its congenial expression, but it transmitted a seriousness during this exchange I'd not previously noticed. I ceded the point and moved on. Leopold/Ramón reached to his right-hand side and lifted onto his lap an attaché case that I didn't know was there. After opening the case, he paused and took another swig of coffee, then handed me a script titled *A Ceaseless Existence*. Leopold/Ramón spoke as I thumbed its pages. Not surprising to me, the film sounded like propaganda. Its focus was an attempted coup The Dictator suppressed to consolidate his power. But I was intrigued and would have said yes had Leopold/Ramón forced me to decide that afternoon. He raised his hand and made eye contact with the waitress, calling her to the table. "Could we have the check, please?" and lifted to his mouth the final bit of coffee, tilting his head backwards and pointing the cup's bottom to the sky. He looked at me and said, "Read the script over the weekend. I'm sure you'll like it. We'll be in contact soon," and with a shrewd, almost imperceptible smile, added, "Our Leader personally believes you are the man to portray him. He is a prudent man. He does not offer his opinions on matters promiscuously." In our ensuing discussions, Leopold/Ramón persuaded me to a choice I'd already decided to make. He must have known this but dutifully carried out his mission. Nothing else had thus far come from making *A Brief Life*. Imagining my remaining years had I passed on this opportunity was simple. The equation was today times infinity. Moreover, during the six weeks of filming, I'd be in the country as a special guest to The Dictator and indulged, feted in ways that could only be provided by a man who commands all of society. And if I never returned to the States, I thought with a little guilt, I'll be famous somewhere. Theresa expressed concern for my safety and hid every inkling of jealousy. "Oliver, I'm not so sure," she told me, "How do you know this isn't a scam and they're sucking you into something dangerous?" She'd heard of the country but was unfamiliar with its ruler and what she learned worried her, but equally true was Theresa believed she was more talented. She thought had fickle life gone another direction Theresa rather than Oliver would be traveling abroad for a last chance at success. That it was me, I admit, felt victorious. Fame, posterity were achievable by me instead of her and this was something she could never un-know. I responded, "I've no idea, Theresa, no earthly idea. Maybe I'll get there and someone will put a bullet in my head or make me a sex slave. But do you really think that'll happen?" She tossed her hands upward as if praising the Lord and muttered, "Sonofabitch." Her conscience had nowhere to hide. But of the many pros and few cons I considered, Greta coming apart might have caused me to stay. I had no reason to believe this was likely, but it was a scenario I often rolled between my fingers. Its remote possibility was intriguing to think about, the lives changed and what her disintegration would have proved about her love for me. Still, with almost one-hundred percent certainty, I would have gone to Ayapaya regardless. My speculations aside, in the lives we actually lived I couldn't allow the emotional distance between us to keep me from leaving. I presumed, because I needed to, her love would be there when I returned, and my presumption was correct. It was more than correct. Absence plus the chance I would be killed made Greta's heart grow especially fonder. Discarding the remnants of my career and life would have been a pointless sacrifice. Because of air travel's peculiarities, I said goodbye to Greta and Theresa before I last saw them. That get-together ended at the front door of the house. We'd spent the day with each other, and here I would love to say, "Like the old times," but it was different. Our old times were happy, not peaceful. But on my final day with them, for the first time more was unsaid than spoken. We hugged, exchanged farewells at the front door. They flashed melancholic smiles when I left and waved listlessly as if the funeral procession of a martyred leader were passing. That evening I finished packing, and because of the front curtains that remained unshut, consumed driblets of Theresa and Greta's goings-on. But when my car arrived before sunrise, neither appeared for a last goodbye.

I landed in crowded, dreary Mexico City and felt suffocated. Its atmosphere was oppressive. People were around and near me at all times, and I desired to stretch my arms and push them out of the world I inhabited. None of the praise I'd read about this centuries-old city appeared truthful. A discouraging first impression, but fortunately, this was a brief layover and I didn't leave the airport. I was greeted by an escort, a young man named Tomás, and shown to my next flight. His, I must add, was the last Ayapayan name I bothered myself to remember. He wore a grey, long-sleeved polo shirt with blue polka dots and black pants; above his left eyebrow was the bulging, inflamed result of a prematurely squeezed pimple. Tomás' eyes watered when he saw me and he turned away, just long enough to wipe them with his wrists. He apologized, "Of course, I'm not as prepared as I thought," then we shook hands and Tomás wrestled what luggage he could from me, managing to do so while sniffling and drying his eyes.

I told him, "No, you don't have to apologize, this must be a very important movie to your country."

With a single, drawn-out breath, Tomás sucked in the snot

running from his nose and nodded, "Indeed, it is. It is," wiped his eyes once more against his forearm, "This way, follow me," he said. He walked a few steps ahead, pulling behind himself the largest of my roll-along luggage and carrying my duffle bag on his back. He was taciturn but would occasionally point at something and talk, though his flawless English was abducted in the busy airport. We walked, I thought, miles, and perhaps, we did. Maybe because my surroundings and life were suddenly unfamiliar, but this airport was louder, more cavernous than any I'd been in. I watched Tomás' back and allowed myself the simple hope that he wasn't as lost as I feared. Nearing the exit, Tomás turned and smiled repeatedly. He was no longer crying and when he looked to me, exposing every tooth in his head, he jutted out his arm as if to say, "See, we're almost there!" Idling curbside was a lustrous black sedan with tinted windows and an Ayapayan flag as its hood ornament. My bitterness for Ayapaya and its citizens is justified a thousand-fold, but their disloyalty can't steal from me the memories of that cerulean sun against a white sky wavering above buildings and parks. The back doors were open. Standing at them were unfairly large, broad-shouldered men in dark, joyless suits equipped with grey, tendrilous earpieces. More of them appeared, taking everything we carried, and hurrying to the street-side door, Tomás smiled and directed me to get in. He sat beside me. The car pulled away and I could tell we were part of a convoy. We moved without stopping, an aquiline siren circled the air. In the States, I would have called Theresa. To share my experience, to gloat, but in Mexico City the idea didn't occur. "Shortly, you'll be in Ayap-aya," Tomás said, "And the entire country will treat you like family, our American cousin, Mr. Apple!" I asked if we were going by car and he laughed. "No, of course not. The Leader sent an airplane for you. We've never had a more important visitor come to our country. Not even the president of the United States would be as important. You'll be treated so well you'll never want to go back," he laughed. "You will love our country. The people are hard-working, very fam-ily oriented. Americans are the same way, yes? Many families live close to each other and gather for meals. We never lose that connection. Many people also do the jobs their parents and grandparents did, follow in the footsteps, as you say. Generations do the same jobs—as possible." Tomás giggled and continued, "Some of the jobs go away, of course. We don't have travel by horse anymore," he said patting the seat, "We have mechanics now. And in some years, we'll have generations of computer programmers. Families passing their knowledge along. It builds …" he paused, and shaking a fist, continued, "strength. In the family is strength. It's a chain. All the links in a chain. Every generation of Ayapayans adds a link." Tomás leaned into me, his fingers interwoven, "That's how you build a country that can't be defeated. Everyone," he said, now pressing his palms against one another, "together. Our Leader's father also ruled. He was a great man." As Tomás spoke, I gave him the uneasy attention you would a person soliciting you on the street. Uninterrupted eye contact, crumpled brow, a desire he'd stop without me having to tell him. But I asked, "Did your father do … what you do?" Tomás answered, "Mr. Apple, some stories get very complicated, of course," and looked outside, "We are here." We'd arrived at a runway and were parking alongside a private jet, a guard and two flight attendants standing at the bottom of its airstairs. The car's passenger got out and opened my door. In front of me, at my feet, a red carpet led to the plane. The flight attendants, who'd been smiling, gasped when they saw me, covering their mouths, and one of them wept. Their uniforms were the cerulean blue of the Ayapayan flag. I heard behind me as I approached, "Mr. Apple, so nice to meet you! Mr. Apple, you will love our country. Mr. Apple, Leopold will meet you in the capital!" I faced Tomás. He was standing on the opposite side of the car with his elbows resting on its roof. Tomás and I waved. Four hands were laid on my arms and back and turned me towards the plane, guided me up its steps.

2

Oliver Apple's face was everywhere. On a wall of the capital city's airport was an enormous banner. He wore a service uniform, ribbons and medals glistening, and looked smilingly into the distance as if foreseeing the country's prosperous future. Similar portraits hung from lampposts and were painted on buildings as my motorcade galloped through the city. I was alone and speechless in the backseat of another sedan. I'd forgotten about my supposed meeting with Leopold/Ramón and my reason for being in Ayapaya. The certainty of knowing, "I'm me and no one else," was evaporating. In less than a day, I'd become the person I was and an imposter. We arrived at a large blue mansion, surrounded by a beautiful, ivory-colored wall, and military guards waved us through its front gate. Along the driveway was an expansive, idyllic green lawn, decorated with trees and prismatic flowers, tended by countless people. The road forked into paths leading to the front and back of the house. I was driven to the backside and into an underground garage then hurried into an elevator with guards at my sides. When those doors opened, I saw a bedroom larger than any house I'd been in, and when they shut behind me, what remained was a false wall. Though I didn't believe it initially, the gold trim along the walls was authentic as were the crystals in the chandeliers. The bed was huge and orgiastic. Rich people actually lived how I imagined. I wasn't one of them but would share their life for six weeks. This sort of optimism is normally followed by a catch, and mine entered that moment. G pushed open the bedrooms' French doors. His entrance, the solemn suit and angelic white shirt, his businesslike air in the second before eye contact evoked the image of a pallbearer. "Mr. Apple," he said, now grinning and showing me to a setup of couches and chairs, "Have a seat, please. My name is …" When the history of my life is written, people will believe he and I were inseparable given his importance to the regime, but I've never remembered his name. From the day we met, I called him G because his face resembled a corpse I saw in a Battle of Gettysburg picture. G was the head of Internal Security and Investigation Services. "Have you enjoyed your stay so far?"

"It's just started. I haven't even had the chance to unpack," which is when I remembered I hadn't seen my luggage since Mexico City. I looked around, twisting at the waist to see if I'd overlooked my suitcases.

"Everything should be in the closets."

"Oh, thank you."

"Yes." G pushed his hands down his legs and grabbed his knees. "Well, right to business." I expected call times or an event to meet my costars, I really wanted to start taking advantage of my role in *A Ceaseless Existence*. I daydreamed celebrations and debaucheries unique to the über-wealthy, but instead G said, "What I have to tell you is a matter of life and death. For Ayapaya and you, to be frank. Our Leader is gravely ill. He is essentially no more, but we cannot tell Ayapayans this. He's a very beloved man, like his father. His father, we call him The Liberator. He gave the care of our nation to his son after our civil war. This government will not survive without him. There is no movie, Mr. Apple. That movie … ," G fluttered both hands above his head. The motion was if he were conjuring what he'd say next rather than searching for the right words. "There is no movie. You want to know why you're here. I'm sure you've noticed your resemblance to The President." I saw a face that had been mine clearer than I'd ever pictured myself. "We are requesting you assume the role of The President publicly. You will make appearances, wave, greet the people," and bringing a finger to his lips, G sternly motioned silence, "but not say a word." I said, "What?" and G responded, "This is very clear, Mr. Apple. You must pay careful attention. You have been brought here to save our nation. That is more important than any movie. We are requesting you—"

"Stop saying 'requesting!'" I yelled, "You're not requesting a goddamn thing, you're forcing me!"

"Mr. Apple, you can do as you please, but we cannot set you

free in the States and certainly not Ayapaya. You are here now and think about what you have to lose."

"There's no fucking movie! I want to go back home!"

G screamed, "There will be no yelling, Mr. Apple! And no swearing! What we are asking of you is more important than a movie. You will help save a nation. Ayapayans are not ready for our Leader's death. You will have the benefit of being thought of as him, but we ask nothing more of you than that. Just pretend. Do you understand what we're requesting, Mr. Apple? Do you understand? Do you understand?" he repeated, "Do you understand? Do you understand? Do you understand? Do you understand? Do you understand? Do you understand? Do you understand? Do you understand? Do you understand? Do you understand? Do you understand? Do you understand? Do you understand? Do you understand? Do you understand?" He might not have repeated the question as many times as I remember, but I was distracted, thinking of the face that had been solely mine. Already the lives of Oliver Apple and The Dictator were becoming mixed-up. Had the airport banner been an image of me? It was difficult to believe otherwise. My brief life was also his. If a twin assumes the existence of another, logically speaking both lives continue … correct? Rivers merging doesn't stop the flow of water. He and I, I and I, he and he remained Oliver Apple and The Dictator. Also, they might have killed me if I refused. "Answer me, Mr. Apple, do you understand?"

"The President is very ill?"

"Mr. Apple, it's important you listen very closely."

"He won't survive long?"

G clutched his legs: "Mr. Apple, what I tell you cannot be repeated. You must keep this secret. Even from yourself. His death is imminent," his jaws expanded and he motioned as though he were about to vomit, "Cancer, this cancer, he's rotting from the inside."

The life that Theresa and Greta were part of concluded that afternoon. And like The Dictator's illness, I foremost needed to conceal its reality from myself. The following morning I walked to a Presidential Palace balcony having shaved my head, scar on my hand concealed with a disturbingly durable makeup, and wearing a thousand-dollar suit. As the other Oliver Apple wilted toward death, thousands stood below me. I'd spent a few hours after my conversation with G studying my doppelgänger's mannerisms. The man had a presidential, in the United States sense, way about himself. Nice posture and barely hidden God complex. I wasn't in power, but I felt powerful. These people were cheering, whistling, yelling, frothing at their mouths as I waved and waved with a Reaganesque tilt of the head. His long-time partner, whom they called The Lady, stood next to me. I saw her seconds before our performance. She was hazel-eyed, frail-looking, the shade of cortadito with thick, black eyeliner. The Lady was in a chic, light-green pant suit, and with a stronger, deeper voice than I anticipated said, "Hello," before taking my arm and walking to the balcony. I considered if becoming The Dictator also meant inheriting his childless relationship and producing a successor, but decided more appropriate times would come for this query. Be that as it may, The Lady and I appeared side-by-side often and without exception she arrived minutes before she was needed. After our hellos, what little more she said was directed at those around us. It was similar to a husband and wife, separated in every way but law, holding it together until their kids are old enough to cope with divorce. We greeted schoolchildren who'd sent us letters at the Presidential Palace. They paraded in front of us, meekly shaking our hands and giving us newer letters they'd written. Our appearances at cultural events were too frequently concerts of their unbearable traditional music, but we moved from car seats to VIP boxes serenaded with applause and notes were un-played until we sat. No evening passed in which the emcee didn't pause between songs to recognize our presence. "Our wonderful President!" "Our immortal Leader!" We'd stand again, waving and smiling, the entire theater applauding. It's odd, given my understandable hatred for Ayapayans, but my happiest experiences were meeting the people, during which

I noticed a difference between the United States and Ayapaya. The US has proud paupers. Most of its citizens would rather ignore a rich person than stand next to him and feel shamefaced about their circumstances. A president's arrival produces hoopla and respect, almost never groveling. But Ayapayans were honest. Their lives could not continue in my presence. Lacking the false self-dignity of their fellow North Americans, Ayapayans were obsequious without shame. Whether alone or with The Lady, I'd arrive unannounced at a grocer or some local tchotchke shop, hugging and shaking hands with people who crowded around. I held babies and picked up youngsters who were pushed to me by their parents. Husbands and wives kissed my hands. Young boys saluted, young girls offered me flowers. Old women, even with The Lady present, grabbed my face and pressed their chapped lips to my cheeks. Elders who were healthy enough clambered to their knees and bowed. I was photographed with families in my arms standing beneath my portrait, which prominently decorated all shops. Much later I discovered how G and other officials worried each time I encountered the public. Secondarily, they feared I would speak and bring the regime down with a single word. Difficult as it is to believe, I never spoke. Mine was a performance of wordless perfection, surpassing the speeches that were deepfaked on Ayapayan TV in Spanish. But their main concern was I'd be assassinated. I assumed my appearances were short because you want the audience desiring more, but they knew among those people might have been my Wilkes Booth. Thinking about those days, it's impossible a killer didn't have the opportunity. Luck and cowardice saved me. Someone fortuitously stepped into his path or my would-be executioner flinched precisely when his opening appeared. I survived then but the streets are filled with assassins now. As the rest of their countrymen did, the Armed Forces would in the end abandon me, too. Dishonorably in its case. But earlier, before treason sickened every part of Ayapayan society, I was adored by soldiers and the military was a backdrop for my most captivating images. I remember wearing my uniform and pinning medals onto chests, their prideful salutes and crying eyes. This happened before and after The Disquiet began, but The Disquiet is what tested the military and made it glorious, in fact. Prior to our troubles, those ribbons and medals cemented The Dictator's rule, The Disquiet gave them meaning in battle. What I also remember is watching our forces and equipment parade down the most well-known boulevard in Ayapaya; sitting at the head of a table made of pink ivory with generals taking my orders; helicoptering above troop formations; watching military operations in real-time on a wall of twinkling monitors. I've mistakenly conflated the two halves of my rule. The rehearsal and the performance. But the international media is doing the same and worse. Scenes of me in uniform are their favorite to replay, but they mix up footage of my phony rule with that of my genuine reign. Regardless, at no point was I omnipotent, contrary to those who chanted, "Fraud!" "Murderer!" in the streets. My first encounter with the limits of earthly power happened in the Presidential Bedroom and also made sense of my interactions with The Lady. This was my initial escapade with a group of The Dictator's favorites, which had been planned to maintain "governmental normalcy." Providing three uninterrupted hours was flattering, but enjoined to murmur nothing more than moans, I tried not to think about the likelihood of surviving that long. Yet, everything was underway when I arrived. I'd taken a sleepless nap in a guest bedroom, anticipating what in reality couldn't be imagined, and entered the Presidential Bedroom with 1, 2, 3, 4, and 5 already unclothed and in progress. I thought, "Early is on time, on time is late, and late is left out of the orgy." Subsequently, having not arrived soon enough to catch the beginning of any X-rated caucus, I was made aware The Dictator preferred to start the action in medias res. Experience persuaded me to this aesthetic point of view. Their mnemonics were obviously headcounts. Sometimes, it was 1, 2, 3, and sometimes 1 and 2. I often couldn't distinguish 1 from the others. The first evening, though, I sheepishly positioned myself on an unoccupied region of the bed. I waited, more uncertain than any period of my life, eventually caressing a foot that belonged to an unseen face. Actors' sex lives aren't what many believe, so this was my first time in bed with more than two women, and those American nights had been eased with marijuana and alcohol. But my anxiety started to lift, I scooted closer. I let go of that ankle and kissed 3, then gave attention to each of them for not entirely selfless reasons. Because no one else acted, I took off my pants and these five young women recoiled at my erection. I'd seen horror on faces like that once: in the bystanders on 9/11. Not before in history had not being able to communicate during an orgy been an issue. I was embarrassed, I was a little frantic, I pressed it against my stomach, and grunting like some neanderthal, angrily waved them from the bedroom. Wrapping themselves in blankets, they ran out and I didn't understand a word of their panic. I believed they'd found my penis underwhelming, a penis which in the United States was at the upper echelons of average. Quibbles in this area were few and because of technique rather than dimensions. Another possibility alarmed me as I considered what happened more, however. Erection averages, I presumed, must be similar between countries, but perhaps I and that other Oliver Apple differed in this way. I summoned G and was sitting on the corner of the bed with a pillow covering myself when he showed up. G didn't sit. "Those women, when they saw me, saw me down here," I said gesturing to my lap, "They freaked out. We couldn't keep going. I threw them out. I might be different from The President. They probably know I'm not him."

G laughed, "Everything works for you, Mr. Apple."

"What?" Was this a question or a statement? "Everything works for me, yes. If I know what you mean."

"Mr. Apple, The President could not be with a woman. For most of his life, this was impossible."

I shook my head, "What?"

"That's your favorite question, Mr. Apple. You should not worry. They were surprised, but they might also believe," facetiously raising his fists, "they've cured The President!"

I chuckled, "I thought it was my size."

"Mr. Apple, a millimeter difference between you and The President and you would still be in the United States. You've done a very good thing," G continued, "No country will survive without a strong leader. A good thing. At a good time … Fools, drunks, Americans, and Ayapayans." His smile was unconvincing.

"A good time?" I asked.

"A good time," he replied. G lowered his head and squinted at the floor, "A good time, Mr. Apple … The President is not with us." I waited, and after a few seconds, G reoriented himself, raised his head, and opened his eyes normally. Then, speaking with his usual tone of voice, "A good time. He has risen. Or it has risen, yes?" and laughed. "I will have them sent back," G told me, "If you're, you're not … tired?"

I understood his implication, what he meant by "tired," and responded with anger, "Of course. Send them back. Nothing happened before."

If those marchers knew The Dictator ruled every piece of Ayapaya but couldn't rule a few inches in his pants, they'd reconsider my alleged guilt for The Disquiet. His death should also be illuminating for them. A tyrant who goes the same way as his people is something less than all-powerful. Were it possible to stop death, The Dictator would've prevented his own. Centuries from now students will learn that death was our turning point. Not my coming here but his dying confidentially. And without G's admission, I might never have known. Either Ayapayans kept secrets better than anyone or the group who knew of two Oliver Apples, two Dictators was immensely small. The shift in my perspective wasn't instantaneous but almost. Before 1, 2, 3, 4, and 5 returned, naked and pawing each other as they crossed the bedroom's threshold, I was starting to think of myself as the true, rightful Dictator. The understudy is a heartbeat from the lead, and my performance had been indiscernible from the "real" man. History casts us in the same role.

The Ayapayan parliament was a sham and I'd always been

contemptuous of its leader. His elfish arms, jowls, and egg-shaped body forced me to call him Agent Frank. This miniature man panted with servility. The deputy leader differed in that she was a woman, was less short, was less fat, and was nicknamed Mr. Beefy. Ayapaya's comedy duo also comprised the second- and third-ranking members of the National-Revolutionary Party for Peace and Prosperity. I was supposed to meet them, a group of parliamentarians, and a token opposition legislator, shake their hands while pictures and video were taken, and leave. They stood to my sides and I crossed my arms to shake Beefy's hand with my left and Frank's hand with my right. Ignorant about whether they spoke English, I subtly tugged their hands downwards and telepathically ordered, "Sit, doggies. Sit." Their eyes moved nervously but their faces did not change, they hesitated but not for long. Without letting go of my hands, Mr. Beefy and Agent Frank genuflected. The others followed. Bowing and painting their faces with smiles as if that had also been ordered. My coup, if that's what people wish to call it, was complete before I returned to the Presidential Palace. They knew I'd fully assumed the role I'd been ordered to play. Their only alternative, G and the rest of them, was revealing how I came to power. My authority could not be turned back now. I was Party Leader, Commander of the Armed Forces, President, Supreme Head of State, Chief Officer of the National Police, The Dictator.

It's especially true of situations like mine that a small group of people should be kept nearby. Your survival requires they be honest and willing to sacrifice themselves. But trusting anyone near me in Ayapaya would have been idiotic. If the choice were my life or theirs, I could predict G and the generals' answers. My bullet-filled, mutilated body dragged behind a pickup truck and left to rot in a city square was nothing if it let those cowards save their reputations and posture as defenders of the country. Bringing Theresa from the United States was also impossible. An American woman living in the Presidential Palace would be suspicious and she'd be overcome with reckless envy when she discovered my carnal obligations. Of the hundreds or thousands of Ayapayans I'd met, only Tomás seemed honorable enough to serve at my side. I had good memories of him. And unlike G or the military brass, he was deferential and would owe his status and future to me. I summoned Tomás from Mexico City to make him an unofficial advisor. For honest patriots, spiritual and political continuity were easily understood and my legitimacy was unquestioned. What he knew of my past didn't affect his seeing me as The Dictator. I remember Teary Tomás grabbing one of my hands and bowing his head when we met again. The young man had never visited the Presidential Palace and looked around as if trying to record every extravagant detail at once. His job was to keep his eyes, his nose, his ears open to threats from within, big or small. If a janitor grumbled about me, I wanted to know. "Of course, Mr. President," he assured, "I will serve honorably. To my final breath," and he stood back and saluted. One person in this deceitful place would give his life for mine. With my watchman in place, act two was taking care of Greta and Theresa. I codenamed it Operation TLC and sent our best spies to the US for this mission. They were joined by an elite intervention team, trained to step in as lethal good Samaritans if my ex-wife or daughter were threatened. Every possible resource was dedicated to their protection. They were observed 24/7 and any data illuminating their unsaid thoughts were monitored. The same was done to anyone they interacted with and, if necessary, anyone those people interacted with. Cash was maneuvered to bank accounts and retirement plans. Daily reports brought me closer to Greta and Theresa than I had been in the States. Nothing more was to be done but rule Ayapaya and this would have been much easier if not for my enemies. I'm certain G and the military withheld information from me. These quislings made sure that if a crisis arose I'd face it partially blind and deaf in one ear. If, that is, the crisis weren't their creation. Looking at the evidence, the story I was told and that's being reported internationally is the real conspiracy theory. They want us to believe the people were inspired to revolt by an old man's self-immolation. Insanity. The transition was smooth.

Our economy was strong. We had peace and stability. My rule was popular. Until The Disquiet began, I was greeted with hugs and kisses by Ayapayans in public. My soldiers and police were loyal and would follow orders like spellbound crusaders. For weeks Tomás was observant and discovered just one plot against me. A group of businessmen had whispered among themselves about a future without The Dictator. When it was uncovered, their plot was in its earliest stages. They'd spit-balled outcomes, ways to protect their interests, but plans of action, possible successors were undiscussed. I had them imprisoned and tried. They mistakenly believed wealth provided immunity. I mistakenly believed leniency would be viewed as strength. Without exception, right-thinking governments punish sedition with death. An artist by birth, I naturally detested finance guys and they were effortlessly executed on my order. Because mining seemed a close blood relative to their monetary chicanery, getting rid of that pathetic executive was also simple. Bullets are convincingly inexpensive. I paused, however, at the farming bigwig. Agriculture I pictured naively as bucolic fields and abundant crops, which affected how I thought of this man. He might have been led astray by richer and more sophisticated individuals. G had advised restraint for all of them, though his prime concern was the opinion of other countries. His eyes were directed towards the United States and Western Europe, but I worried about Mexico. It was too big and too close to be trusted. I rejected his advice with the others but was persuaded to it in this final case. That honcho received life in prison, and I should have followed with G and the generals. But I was unable to learn enough about ISIS leadership and the military chain of command to act. Who would I replace them with? Dependence is a state of total weakness. And conveniently, a month later, a country at peace with itself and its neighbors had devolved into social breakdown.

Explaining The Disquiet's genuine causes would be speculation. Details are securely buried in the minds of its plotters. However, the looking-glass reality disseminated by forces in the Ayapayan government and gobbled up and transcribed by the international media starts in a local market. Here a disheveled and, one assumes, mentally ill old man was panhandling. According to the story we're given, his shop had been forced out of business, as though someone making a better product were a crime. But as he must have known, this behavior was strictly disallowed. Numerous channels existed for people in actual need. Real poverty was unheard of in Ayapaya before The Disquiet. His illegal begging in the streets is clue one about the event's veracity. Members of our beautifully uniformed, and until-then loyal, police forces ordered him to leave the market, but he refused. After ignoring more warnings and resisting their attempts to expel him, he was finally made to obey and arrested. Owing to the humanity of our police, the old man spent a single night in jail and was released the next morning. But so disheartened and humiliated with having been punished for his crimes apparently, the old man returned to the market and self himself on fire. Anyone willing to think critically spots the setup. I suspect elements in Ayapaya recruited this hapless old man from another country and paid his family a lot of money after his suicide. The well-being of his kin was the destruction of this nation. Protests, spontaneous and without direction from officials here or elsewhere they want us to believe, started after the old man's death. I believed they'd tire and leave the streets, and G agreed. He recommended large, visible National Police contingents to keep order but the time had not arrived for stronger means. Yet, they became larger, as though what had been paid to the old man's relatives was replicated for millions, and soon protests were in front of the Presidential Palace. G, whose concerns about "international opinion" were less suspicious than they should have been, continued to counsel patience. My generals could not agree. I remember them by their branches. Army and Navy advised a strong hand, the Air Corps did not. Speaking privately, Tomás said, "I don't want to see my country destroyed." He wept, "I don't want to see my country destroyed." Penetrating the palace's walls, I could hear, "Murderer Out!" "Food and money!" "Murderer Out!" "Food and money!" I did what my situation required and ordered police to clear the streets. I don't know how many were killed or injured those first nights. Quite a few but obviously not enough. They kept returning, day and night, shouting, marching, shutting down much of the country, attacking police and burning buildings, throwing bottles at the Presidential Palace (The Lady, due back from her profligacy in Paris, had instead galvanized the rioters by banishing herself to the Ritz). G suggested I get tougher but also hold Ayapaya's first presidential elections. "And if I lose?"

"These people are not Ayapaya," he said, waving his hand toward the streets. We could hear them chanting. Sirens. Bangs. I heard, unmistakably, fires burning somewhere. "These savages are a minority. The people are with The Party. They support you."

"And if I lose?"

"Elections will show you are dedicated to reform. The world will tell them to leave the streets. The opposition is disorganized. Almost nothing. You will win."

"And if I lose?"

He answered calmly, "A peaceful transition can be assured. Certainly, Mr. President."

I waited, anticipating G might amend what he said or offer something different. Neither him nor the generals spoke until I said, "And what happens to me?"

"We still have many friends, Mr. President. Exile is possible."

He emitted words as if his were the most rationale utterances on Earth. "Exile is possible." "Exile is possible." I don't know what G conceived, but my pathway from Ayapaya led to the United States. And if I were to return home, I needed victory. Winners dictate conditions. Terms are meted to losers. G's idea wasn't the best plan, it was the only plan. I wish those marchers knew how dependent I was on a man who now poses as a repentant bureaucrat and reformer. My next steps could have been ordered and carried out by him. I mobilized the Ayapayan Armed Forces. Our infantry, our commandos, our sea forces, our bombers, and our fighter jets. We generated a statement, which aired "live," in which I expressed my solidarity with the silent majority that had remained loyal. I said Ayapaya would not yield to terrorists and "the streets would be fumigated for these rats as we do for any others." The latter sentence I specifically asked to be included. In my denouement, I announced elections would occur in days. Ayapayans would be given two choices: yes or no to my leadership. I gave the protestors a sunrise deadline to disperse. Reckoning my leniency with the agriculture executive had given the wrong impression, he was executed. But when I awoke from a solid eight hours of sleep, their violence continued. While I slept a government building was destroyed and neighborhoods had ringed themselves with tires and trash bins and cars. Their makeshift "defenses" were obliterated in the military's first attack. I watched, my eyes shifting excitedly from screen to screen, as we began pushing into these areas, bombs exploding, retaking neighborhoods. I started laughing uncontrollably. I'd known intuitively, it was part of my being, that accomplishing whatever goal you desired was essentially a matter of will. One's readiness to endure is in most cases life's secret, and nothing exhibited this more than day after day watching these Ayapayan scumbags forced into submission. Elections had gone well, too. The yeses had won 98.8 percent of the vote and within days, after the results were certified, my authority would be unquestioned. From there I could magnanimously renounce the office and secretly return to the United States if I chose. Here, again, though, my fortunes shifted. I was told by G that our "allies" had issued statements of concern and some elements in those countries were demanding they withdraw support. G recommended I halt operations and from my "position of strength" offer to share power with the opposition. If not, stories might soon appear in the international press of who I'd been months ago. I did what he suggested. Forty-eight hours later Tomás reported half the National Police, our best Army and Navy units, and much of the Air Corps were prepared to mutiny. The *New York Times* article was headlined, "American Actor Seizes Power in Ayapaya, Triggers Revolt."

<u>3</u>

Proving himself the most honest Ayapayan was easy, he was born in a land of mendacious people. But Tomás also proved himself to be an honest man without regard to country. I would be dead without him. G had stopped answering my calls, and through a bedroom curtain parted with a peace sign, I could see tanks and soldiers maneuvering towards the palace. The loyal resistance was weakening, deserting, or pissing themselves. Hours after Army took the airwaves and hours before he seized the Presidential Palace, Tomás and a small group of sympathizers helped me escape. With me hidden in car trunks, we moved between safehouses and empty, bombed-out buildings squaring off with rodents for whatever food we found or had with us. Just once did Tomás approach betrayal. That evening we were staying in a small, four-room house, which even with a few guards, felt unprotected. Bullet holes pockmarking its walls and shattered windows, the collapsing roof were expected, but celebratory gunfire and shouting were too close in this instance. My paranoia that any day at any second I'd be captured, bound, tortured, killed, and strung up was particularly intense. Tomás entered the room where I was lying awake on a concrete floor, covered by a thin blanket, in the barren glow of candle flame and starlight. "We must leave before sunrise," he said, "We can get through the northern checkpoint if we do. It's not certain. But we can." Without fail and with complete sincerity, he told me his tactical plans as if I understood what any of it meant or could offer disagreement. In reality, I am a wanted man in a foreign country and, for the moment, being carried along by whatever schemes he puts together.

I pointlessly replied, "I'll be ready."

"Of course," he answered, conveniently leaving on the floor next to me one of his pistols.

Tomás knew I did not carry a gun. I loathed that appendage to my old military uniform. Not to mention the occasions when I had to wield pistols and rifles and shoot them in the air. Guns are heavy and offend my sense of self. They are instruments of death and I could never aim and fire one at a person. Living by the sword obviously invites the hellacious pain of dying by one, too. He knew this but sensed my unspoken dread. He was also afraid for himself. If I am captured, those who aided and abetted a foreigner and so-called war criminal are his accomplices. Suicide was a simple answer. And I imagine he might've portrayed himself as a murderer and saved his name in history. Tomás was respectful at least and implied his fatalism rather than speak it. Yet, when he reappeared before sunrise, I was alive and the gun unfired. We were smuggled through that northern checkpoint and now continue toward the Ayapayan border. His plan, which is mine, too, is sneaking into Guatemala and concealing ourselves among northbound migrants until we reach the US-Mexico border. Here is, I suspect, where I'll have to leave my Ayapayan Sherpa behind. When we reach the United States, I'll reveal the face the world has seen a million times and trust in the uniqueness of my birthright. Our first try is in hours. We're preparing, waiting in what had been a family's home. I've shaved for the first time in more than a week, been given a dark wig that runs to my shoulders and covers my face, an oddly radiant lipstick, and am wearing a filthy wool dress that covers my arms and legs. The dress's shade of dark orange would be nice if not for the circumstances. My sinistral scar, as though it were a McFly sibling, has begun its reappearance, too, and as it was for them, my future is also in the past. Picturing what had been in this abandoned, crippled house reminds me of life before Ayapaya. Dirtied family photos and broken possessions are scattered everywhere. But, like me, they took what they could. My lone solace is the final report I received from Operation TLC. I carry it with me, rereading and thinking about Greta and Theresa's love and imagining how much we'll hug and cry when I return.

Shaun Rouser is a writer based in Chicago. He is the author of *Family Affair* (Red Bird Chapbooks), *The Chef Connection* (Alien Buddha Press), and *Arthur, August 2018* (Anxiety Press). More of his fiction has appeared in *Colloquium*, *RIC Journal*, *The Rupture*, and *deLuge Journal*. His one-act play, *American Meat,* was published in *Fleas on the Dog.* He previously co-founded and served as co-editor-in-chief of online arts and humanities journal *The Blackstone Review,* where he also contributed fiction and non-fiction.

MORE ROADSIDE PRESS TITLES:

By Plane, Train or Coincidence
Michele McDannold

Prying
Jack Micheline, Charles Bukowski and Catfish McDaris

Wolf Whistles Behind the Dumpster
Dan Provost

Busking Blues: Recollections of a Chicago Street Musician and Squatter
Westley Heine

Unknowable Things
Kerry Trautman

How to Play House
Heather Dorn

Kiss the Heathens
Ryan Quinn Flanagan

St. James Infirmary
Steven Meloan

Street Corner Spirits
Westley Heine

A Room Above a Convenience Store
William Taylor Jr.

Resurrection Song
George Wallace

Nothing and Too Much to Talk About
Nancy Patrice Davenport

Bar Guide for the Seriously Deranged
Alan Catlin

Born on Good Friday
Nathan Graziano

MORE ROADSIDE PRESS TITLES:

Under Normal Conditions
Karl Koweski

The Dead and the Desperate
Dan Denton

Clown Gravy
Misti Rainwater-Lites

Walking Away
Michael D. Grover

All in a Pretty Little Row
Dan Provost

These Are the People in Your Neighbourhood
Jordan Trethewey

They Said I Wasn't College Material
Scot Young

Radio Water
Francine Witte

And Blackberries Grew Wild
Susan Mickelberry

Licorice Heart
Miles Budimir

Disposable Darlings
Todd Cirillo

Full Moon Midnight
Belinda Subraman

Innocent Postcards
John Pietaro

Cistern Latitudes
James Duncan

MORE ROADSIDE PRESS TITLES:

Another Saturday Night in Jukebox Hell
Alan Catlin

Abandoned By All Things
Karl Koweski

Ain't These Sorrows Sweet?
Lauren Scharhag

Gregory Corso: Ten Times a Poet
Lauren Scharhag

She Throws Herself Forward to Stop the Fall
Dave Newman

We Don't Get to Write the Ending
Aleathia Drehmer

These Many Cold Winters of the Heart
Ryan Quinn Flanagan

Things You Never Knew Existed
Josh Olsen

Maze: stories
Jennifer Juneau

Green Roses Bloom for Icarus
Hiromi Yoshida

Apocalypsing
Jason Anderson